LOVE BY CHANCE

LOVE BY CHANCE

MANSI KASHYAP

Srishti
PUBLISHERS & DISTRIBUTORS

Srishti Publishers & Distributors
A unit of AJR Publishing LLP
212A, Peacock Lane
Shahpur Jat, New Delhi – 110 049
editorial@srishtipublishers.com

First published by
Srishti Publishers & Distributors in 2022

10 9 8 7 6 5 4 3 2 1

Dedicated to
my school-time memories
from Faith Academy, New Delhi.

Acknowledgements

When serendipity strikes you, the blood in your veins sings and dances, especially when you are a teenager. It is never too soon to receive what you wish for and never too late to ask for it.

This book was purely written from sheer nostalgic memories of my teen years that I cherish to this day. I would like to thank from the bottom of my heart, all the teenagers that I have interacted with while writing this novel.

There are a few more people who I am grateful to for playing a significant role in my journey.

Ridheiy Verma, for spending your evenings with me to discuss teenage issues and giving me wonderful ideas while we sat next to the swimming pool.

#MySupportiveFamily, that always encouraged me to grow in whatever I chose to do with my career. I was always blessed with your tremendous support.

Vijay Das for writing songs for my book. #Hope and other songs written in this book are originals penned by him.

Thanks to Sudo @sudotsd for writing the #Mom poem for this book on such short notice.

Michael Shine from Texas, for writing the closing lines for my book based on the title when he should have been shopping for #BabyOnTheWay.

My brother Anand Narula for designing my company logo. Special credits to Annie for writing the amazing opening lines for this book based on the title, when she was fasting for Ramadan.

Mrs Sara Varkey, my favourite teacher at school. You rock, and you inspire me always. Anirban Roy, my proofreader from Vietnam – your words always bring positivity.

I thank Arjun Randhawa for helping me out with the early discussions about the story and suggesting changes.

Thanks, Suhail Mathur from The Book Bakers, for pitching my book to Srishti Publishers.

And last but not least, to all those school kids who unknowingly inspired me to write this book. Those who are exceptional in their way; dealing with their frivolous, sometimes uncontrolled lives, and still holding on to it.

Prologue

Ting

This is the second call for all passengers boarding Delta Airlines flight headed to New York. All passengers proceed to gate number 5. The flight is now boarding.

Do not leave your baggage unattended. If you see any unattended bags, please inform the security staff immediately. Thank you.

I couldn't stop admiring the voice of the lady making the announcement. I looked over to see passengers around gate number 5. They picked up their cabin baggage and other paraphernalia and started walking towards the boarding gate. My flight still had some time.

I was sitting at a barstool in Café 24, sipping my usual frappé. The anxiety of going to a new place filled my veins faster than caffeine in my blood. Out of sheer exhilaration, I sang.

'Skylights low may be dim, I wait. My heart's pounding more than ever before.'

An older man speaking over a call looked at me and sang along, 'It's dawn or maybe a rise.'

An English guy sipping his coffee joined in. 'Who cares? Just take it as it flows, enjoy the mystery that ravels.'

The girl with a tattoo sitting next to the bar chimed, 'Go where your urge takes you, take the road less travelled.'

A police officer passing by couldn't resist. 'But be watchful, don't lose your grip…in one moment you know your life can flip.'

I smiled and sang, 'It's gloomy outside. I hold good memories, yet some to forget.'

The air hostess rolling her trolly bag smiled as she added, 'The sky is our home, and we dwell in the clouds.'

The waitress at my table also sang along, 'Break away, feel free, float in love so much I wish.'

The housekeeping boy added, 'Unfulfilled dreams, hopelessness, and fake smiles are all I see.'

A lady on the wheelchair sang, 'All's well, have faith and be that drive you.'

I turned towards the housekeeping boy and continued, 'Let love be your strength, let hope be your spur.'

My dad surprised me, 'I see you the lone one shining in my view, the only one that matters.'

I beamed as I sang, 'Give me light! Show me the way, as I dream, I wonder, I pray for a brighter way.'

Everyone around sang together. 'Guide her, take care of her. Find the new beginning for her.'

The English guy dropped his hat. The kids continued swinging their legs sideways as they watched. The guy at the bar thumped on the glass with a stirrer. Everyone swung their arms in the air as they sang and danced together. And the sound of claps filled the air.

#GameOfFamilies

Ladies and Gentlemen, as we start our descent, please make sure your seat backs and tray tables are upright and your seat belt is securely fastened.

As the pilot announced the arrival in twenty minutes, I tried to straighten my back and stretch my legs. I felt numb in my feet. I had been sitting like that for eight hours and fifteen minutes.

I had managed to take a nap for an hour in between, read a book on my kindle, played video games and listened to Maroon 5 songs. Then, I looked at my brother sitting next to me. He was playing PUBG that arrested his existence.

I smiled and then looked out of the plane window, leaning on my side, watching a powdery blue azure sky. The sun rays sharply fell on my mom and gave a canary yellow hue to her hair. It was a clear sky, giving me the hope that the next phase of my life was going to be different.

The gloomy, grey skies of London, the unpredictable rains and strong winds could give me #IWokeUpLikeThis look at any given time of the day!

Sometimes, I loathed the grey skies because it always restricted me indoors and I am kind of an outdoor girl.

Oh! I forgot to introduce myself.

Hi, I am Jasmeet Sethi, your regular #GirlNextDoor. Good in studies, bad at sports, good at helping underdog friends, bad at bullying, good at making genuine friends, bad at ignoring, a good listener and bad at dating. Yeah, I mean it. It just never worked out for me.

There was this guy in my previous school whom I dated for barely seven days. On the seventh day, we went for a drive to the countryside, listening to good music. Suddenly, he stopped the borrowed car that his dad had given him and came closer. The moment he kissed me, I knew that was my last day with him.

The next day I landed in school, hearing the news from some of my classmates that he told everyone I admitted to him being a good kisser and was all over him during the whole drive. I had never felt the need to slap somebody before. That was when I broke up with him. And that was when I started having trust issues with boys in general.

I might seem like a confident little girl who's bold and ready for any trials in life, but sometimes I dread changes like making new friends, switching schools, obnoxious relatives and the list never ends. I just like to be in my bubble. I like all things around me to remain as they are. It just makes me a bit more agreeable with life, enveloped in my protective and comforting way. Period!

◆

Another announcement was made by the beautiful flight attendant who managed to look fresh, even after a long flight.

Her lips were moving perfectly while she announced.

Ladies and gentlemen, welcome to Indira Gandhi International Airport, New Delhi. The local time is 11:30 a.m., and the temperature outside is 38 degrees.

I saw my dad getting up, trying to get our cabin baggage. My dad worked for a biomedical company in East London. He is smart, intellectual and very flexible; which means he listens to mom more than anyone else in our house. He has a different side too. I would like to call it a no-nonsense side. The most disciplined man I have ever come across.

We settled in London when I was two. But now we are here, in New Delhi, to live in our own house with my grandparents. My granny had not been keeping well since last year, so my dad decided we should all move to India to be with them. Our families are very strong and closely knit, and we are always there for each other. Every summer vacation, we visit Delhi. Sometimes, my grandparents visited us in London. But now granny is very ill to see anyone, so people are seeing her more.

If I take a trip down my memory lane, I recollect my granny being very active when we were kids. She stayed with us for eight months when my brother Monty was born. She picked me up from my school every single day, took me to park in the evenings and helped make dinner at night. And granny did all that whole-heartedly. At night, after everyone went to sleep, we would chat a bit before going to bed. Now I would see her again and I was glad.

My grandmother is an ultra-fine woman until her daughter screws up everything for us. Granny doesn't pay much heed till the time her daughter provokes her to a make-me-mad-by-gossiping level. That's where I hate my relatives. They just talk nonsense all the time.

My mom says it is a power game. But, what power game?

I have heard about *Game of Thrones* and *The Sacred Games*, what is it with this #GameOfFamilies now? Aunt Barkha says grandma loves my mom more than her and grandma says there is no truth in that. My mom says because all of us take care of granny, aunt shouldn't even poke her nose into our family matters!

Dad doesn't bother much. He has adapted himself to all this family politics. I don't understand him when he agrees with mom, and then, he agrees with aunt Barkha as well! Anyway, 'Game of Families' it is!

This is the Sethis for you. Welcome to my world!

#ThingsToLookForwardTo

'Namaste sir! Namaste madam!' Mahesh, our driver, greeted us outside the airport and loaded our bags in the boot.

Mahesh has been working for grandpa for almost eight years now. He has three daughters back in his village in Bihar. He is honest, dad says. The only thing that I feel awkward or maybe funny about Mahesh bhaiya is that he is a calm person most of the time until he sees a driver of a small car.

I mean we own a BMW and a Mercedes, and believe me! I am not making a spectacle of our lavish life. All I am pointing at is how having a big car changes everything.

As soon as we hit the road, Monty fell asleep. I looked out of the window and was blinded by the intense sun, the searing heat, the extreme weather, deafened by the honking of cars and overwhelmed by the traffic snarls. NH8 and the Cyber Hub reminded me of the Financial Centre in Canary Wharf in East London and the DLR metro going around, carrying office-goers to their destinations.

I wondered what it would be like, working for one of these companies one day! My eyes gleamed at the thought. It's still a long way to go. I am only sixteen and in eleventh grade. For now, I should be more concerned about my new school.

Monty woke me up first when the driver pulled over outside our gate. 'You were snoring!' he proclaimed. I looked at him in disbelief while coming out of the car and shrugged.

'No, really!' he added with a cheeky smile.

I took my bag and started walking towards the gate, but turned back to reply, 'You should mind your own business, you nerd!'

'Shut up, you psycho!'

At this, my mom cried out, 'Stop fighting, you both!' She was always tired of our fights. But I believe sibling fights are as important as having breakfast every day. We find each other irritating sometimes, but we love each other.

◆

As we reached home, my granny sauntered and we greeted her. I hugged her tight. Her frail body broke my heart a little. Her cheeks had gone inside, and her slender hands looked clumsy. It was like somebody had taken some air out of a balloon. But, I was relieved to see that she could still walk.

'How are you, ma?' my dad gave her a big hug and kissed her temples. The moment mom bowed down to her, granny too bowed down a little, and their heads bumped with each other by mistake.

'Hope you are okay, ma?' Mom got a little worried about the bump.

Granny grasped mom's arm and then hugged her. 'How are you Manju?'

'I am fine, ma.' Mom finally smiled, and her fearful expressions disappeared.

We all sat together in the living room. Grandpa was sitting on his rocking chair, devouring the newspaper. He reads it in the morning with his *chai*, and this ritual goes on until lunchtime.

Lakshmi, our housekeeper, came with chai and some cookies. She takes good care of Granny and also cooks yummy *parathas*. I call her #LoyalBindiLadyKiller.

Lakshmi wears a cotton saree and sports a big red *bindi* on her forehead. She told me once, 'All married women must wear a red bindi as a symbol of marriage. I wondered how she would feel if I took her to London one day.

I don't drink tea, so I decided to stroll in our garden. I noticed a few changes since last year. Lakshmi must have taken good care of the garden. The well-manicured lawn and neatly trimmed plants gave it a healthy look.

The flowering plants of china roses, bougainvillea, night blooming jasmines looked pretty. We call it *raat ki rani* because its flowers only open at night. I was wonderstruck by this fact when grandpa first told me.

As I was observing my peaceful surroundings, I saw Lakshmi coming with a tray of coffee. I thanked her and looked around. It was a strip of road lined with cars and gulmohar trees. It brought back loads of memories of our good times spent in Delhi.

I started wondering what Samar must be up to. You must me thinking who is this brand new character in my story?

Samar Suri has been my summertime buddy here. The Suris live next door. Mom and aunty are good friends. Our families go to the city club together whenever we are here. We always have so much fun together. We have long swimming sessions, followed by cocktails by the poolside, chatting, laughing and eating brunch together at the club.

The two families are inseparable!

Samar is smart, witty and uncluttered. He is well-groomed. He looks very dapper, unlike the other ragged boys his age. His sharp features, well-styled hair, a perfect nose and thin lips make him stand out. His smile is cool and subtle. I have always had a summertime crush on him when we came here for vacation, let's say.

That day, I couldn't find him around. It was just their gardener trimming the plants.

◆

My mom called out from inside the house, 'Jessi, come inside and take some rest!' It was a long flight, and she insisted I take a nap.

'Okay, Mom,' I replied lazily. Plus, Delhi heat made me super lazy.

I took a quick shower and rested on my bed. I started thinking about the new school I would be going to, but the jet-lag started disorienting my body rhythms. My parents were exhausted too, but since there were things to do and people to see, they were quite excited to be here in Delhi.

I didn't have any of those. I mean, things to do and people to see! So I dozed off to sleep.

◆

When I woke up, it was already dinner time. Lakshmi had made us some nice dinner because my family likes to eat simple home-cooked food most of the time. Only when we go out for dinners, we try different cuisines. My dad likes the food cooked by my mom.

When she was working in London, she used to cook and freeze food for dad because of the lack of time. A lot of times, everyone in the family forgot there was food in the freezer, and we used to end up ordering from a nearby deli. Then at night, when mom used to return from work, she would get ballistic about the whole thing as to why we ordered outside food when there was enough in the freezer.

Lakshmi had made some potato curry and cucumber *raita* with the aromatic *basmati* rice. Mom made some macaroni and cheese for Monty and me. We were overwhelmed. It had been comfort food for both of us and nostalgic to our days back in London. Macaroni-and-cheese has always been a coping mechanism during our tough times at school, exam pressure and late-night studies.

Monty usually reports late at the dinner table, and he did that yet again.

'No iPads on the dining table, please!' Dad said in his authoritative voice. I told you my dad is a no-nonsense kind of dad, didn't I?

'First, you keep *your* phone down!' Grandad immediately ordered my dad.

Didn't I tell you my grandad too is a no-nonsense kind? Maybe not! But you would realize soon. It's a gene thing. Our family has a big problem of correcting each other. It's a significant issue when everyone thinks they are the best.

Monty went back to his room to keep the iPad and dad's phone. By the time he was back, all of us had already started eating.

'Life's truly bliss!' Monty sighed contentedly.

'Jessi, you should try some homemade curry,' my grandad suggested.

'Maybe I will try tomorrow, grandad. Right now, I just want to savour this yummy macaroni and cheese.' I grinned.

◆

After dinner, we all sat down in the living room. Grandma wanted to take some rest after the little bumpy accident that happened in the morning, so she went to her room to sleep. As much as I wanted to chat with her in her room, I realised that she needed rest.

My grandad works as per a fixed schedule every day. I have never seen him out of this error-free, precise, flawless schedule ever in my life! His early morning walks in the neighbourhood, his punctuality towards daily chores, well-timed baths, worship time, breakfast time – it is exemplary. At night, post-dinner time, he likes to watch some news channel for exactly fifteen minutes and then goes to sleep. He also prefers to be independent. For instance, I have always seen him making his bed. I know this sounds petty, but at his age, small things like these matter a lot.

'You should sleep on time and get up early every day!' Grandad muttered as soon as he spotted us, tapping away on our iPad screens; our favourite post-dinner-amuse-ourselves-leisure-time.

'Grandad, we have already slept so much during the day,' I tried to reason out with him.

'Okay, tomorrow you both are coming for a morning walk with me, so get ready at 6:00 a.m.' He declared while adjusting his glasses.

I thought there was no point arguing, so I replied, 'Okay. Hope you sleep well, grandad!' I hugged him before he left for his room. You know, I adore my family, no matter how unreasonable they are at times.

◆

I was comfortably sitting on an olive green Lounge chair in the living room and listening to "Payphone" by Maroon 5. Monty was sitting on a comfy floor cushion square, listening to some heavy metal (I guess because I could feel the bass frequencies blowing out a little too much from his headphones.)

'I hope you remember you have to wake up early in the morning to go with grandad?' He joked.

'Not just me... he meant both of us!' I broke the news to him.

'You are such a sadist!' he grinned.

'Well, tomorrow is going to be an eventful day. Early morning walk with Hitler Dadaji and then, dad told me we are going to check out some schools tomorrow as admission dates are drawing to a close.'

'Not tomorrow! He told me the day after. Tomorrow we are going to hang out in M-main.'

'Oh Yeah, why don't you sleep then?'

'Yeah, I am about to crash. You have a good night Monty.'

'Yeah, sleep tight and don't let the bed bugs bite!' he giggled on this nursery rhyme that we used to sing together and then went back to his music as I climbed the stairs to my bedroom.

#NuancesOfGrowingUp

I was huffing and puffing by the time we reached home. I remembered the story of the three little pigs that I had read when I was in first grade. The wolf went to the first pig's house and said, 'I will huff and I will puff, and I will blow your house away.' The wolf must have had the morning walk with my grandad on a super sultry and hot day in Delhi!

I would instead prefer a gym over going with grandad on a morning walk. I must say it was quite energy-sucking.

Monty had outwitted me in the morning. He was smart enough to be in the washroom when grandad came knocking at his door. And everybody knows that grandad doesn't wait for anyone. He gave me a smug wink when I entered the house. I was sweating, so I ignored him and headed straight towards the shower. On my way to my room, I could see through the glass door that mom and dad were enjoying their coffee with Samar's parents. I decided to say a quick hi!

'Hello uncle, hello aunty! How are you doing?' I smiled at them.

'We are fine, Jessi! Just talking with your dad about school options. Come back quickly so we can discuss more,' Aunty said.

'Sure, I will be back in ten minutes. Lakshmi, can I please get a coffee?' I requested. She nodded and smiled. I quickly grabbed my towel and walked upstairs.

When I returned, I sat next to mom on the arm of the couch and grabbed my coffee in one hand. That's my usual style to sit on the armrest of the sofa. Their little bullmastiff started rolling around me, and I freaked out totally. Last time, it was a pug. I am not allergic to dogs or anything, but I just psych out when they try to lick my clothes or start smelling me!

'Last time it was a pug, aunty?' I asked.

'He was autistic and a little mentally unstable, darling. He had to be handled by a dog psychologist, so for now, we adopted this one. This one is my new baby.'

'Jeez, now dogs have autism? I thought only humans could get suicidal thoughts.

The dog started licking aunty's manicured hands. It took me a while to digest that PDA.

'We are celebrating Plucky's birthday next month at the clubhouse. Please, you all have to be there,' Suri aunty said proudly.

What would I get as a gift for him? I had all sorts of weird ideas I can't even write here. I saw a t-shirt online once with a caption "I work hard so that my dog can have a better life!" I think if mom allows it, I can give that to aunty.

'So, we were just discussing Samar's school, the curriculum and everything else, Jessi,' my mom said, shaking me out of my reverie.

'Oh, okay,' I acknowledged while taking a sip.

'We need to make a quick decision about the school,' Dad added.

'Whoa, I didn't know getting admission here in Delhi is such a big task!' I raised my eyebrows in disbelief.

'Yes, it is darling,' Mrs Suri smiled. One thing you would notice about Suri aunty is that she calls everyone 'darling'. From her dog to her son to her husband!

Mrs Suri is quite well-informed. She works as a program director in Fellowship Health Resources in New Delhi. Also, she is well-acquainted with the educational system here and has contacts with renowned educational institutions and schools. Her husband, Mr Suri is a senior director, Finance and Operations, in a US-based company. He manages the advanced level and professional internal auditing work. Uncle Suri travels to the US several times a year. My dad and uncle have known each other since their university days. They graduated from UCLA.

It was a working day, so the Suris left. My dad already had breakfast with Suri uncle, so he too got ready for work.

Dad reports to his new office now and heads the research and development division in a UK based biomedical firm called Genepro. My mom works from home most of the time now. A graduate from Stanton University in the UK, she is a motivational speaker. When she was working, she used to hold workshops on self-confidence, motivation and work-life balance. Now she is implementing all her principles by maintaining a work-life balance. However, one thing that she finds hard to balance is her on and off migraine attacks.

Last time we had a parent-teacher conference when her migraine attack hit her badly! I remember, out of hundreds of good things that the teacher spoke about me, mom only remembered the worst one, where I slept during the history lecture. Under normal conditions, mom would not even have bothered about such things, but during her migraine, her nerves get 100% *extra boost* to give me a #NerveAttack.

The topic of sleeping in the class continued until her cycle came, and finally, she calmed down.

I am telling you all this because, when we think we kids are growing up, the parents start to act like teenagers. It is like hormones are attacking teenagers and parents together. So I pray to god that when I get my PMS, please don't give mom a migraine attack because then, the house will be a mess.

If you don't understand what I am saying, then I pray to God that he makes you a girl in your next lifetime.

#BumpingIntoSamar

Faster Fries in the neighbourhood was my go-to place whenever I was in Delhi. It's just walking distance from our house.

As we were nearing the cafe, the smell of the fries made our mouth water. The menu on the aesthetic black chalkboard invited us. Monty and I split a Ham and Swiss sandwich as it was huge.

'I will be back in a minute,' I said before leaving Monty with his iced tea and the sandwich.

'Hi, can I have some mustard, please?' I told the girl behind the counter, and she handed me a squeezy bottle of mustard sauce. As I turned after thanking the girl, I bumped into Samar.

'Hi, how are you?' The words escaped my mouth as soon as I saw him.

'Hey, I'm good, Jess. Nice to see you! Come, let's sit somewhere,' he replied.

'I came with Monty. Join us on that table next to the pillar… the very last on the left. Yeah,' I pointed out to him.

'Okay, let me just pay and I'll join you guys.' He turned back to the counter and paid for his croissant and golf coffee.

After a minute, he joined us.

'Hey, dude!' Monty and Samar gave each other a #BoysHug. You know what that is, right? Not too clingy like we girls do and not too formal like the adults.

'How are you, bro?' Samar asked Monty.

'Just getting used to the heat,' Monty whined.

'And this shall pass too,' I preached.They both burst into laughter.

'What?' I asked, perplexed at their reaction.

'You know she always has a unique way of dealing with things, right?' Monty was taking a dig at me.

'Chill, man! We all have our coping mechanisms, and we will have many occasions to enjoy the outdoors. Delhi is not as bad as you think. Let's plan to play Xbox at my place sometime. What say?' Samar said.

'Yeah, that way you guys can beat the heat.' I winked at Monty.

'Jessi can join us too! I mean if she likes,' Samar blushed at me.

'Nah, thanks. I am always well-placed with my books and music.' I smiled at Samar.

'I don't enjoy Xbox games much, but we can all go together to the city club on weekends and have fun with the family. Samar, what do you say?' I added.

'Yes, of course. Next weekend is done!' His eyes lit up as he said that.

Like I mentioned before, we always longed to go to the city club whenever we were here. It's bliss. In London, it's freezing most of the time, but in peak summers, we did hang outdoors. We longed for the sun to come out. We all used to bag a spot on the top deck of London's river boats and relax with the wind in our hair.

In summers, London gets transformed into a whole new city. The parks get packed with sunbathers. I remember playing with Monty in Hyde Park and watching street performers juggling, acrobating their way to glory. My favourite part of these outings was to see the musicians perform live in the piazza in Covent Garden or watching a Shakespeare play in the open-air theatre at Regent Park.

But now, I am here, and this is going to be my home for now, until who knows when!

#CheckingOutDelhiSchool

The next day, when we were over our so-called jet lags, Dad and I went to visit Hibiscus Valley School, that was recommended to us. We had to wait for almost an hour to meet the counsellor. There was a huge rush of parents filling up the forms and meeting the school staff, occasionally bumping into one another. With the admission dates closing and limited seats, the staff looked nervous and disoriented, unlike the marvellous facade. The flawless infrastructure did not match the mismanaged staff. Anyway, when the lady at the front desk finally saw our foreign passport details, she came rushing towards us.

'Sorry to keep you waiting for so long, please come inside. Yes, this way please,' she ushered us inside a small but classy cabin and shut the door behind us.

The counsellor was seated on the other side. She wore club master inspired vintage style spectacles that failed to hide her big protruding eyes. She picked up the phone and dialled two buttons before saying, 'Two coffees.'

'Thank you, but we are actually in a hurry,' my dad conveyed to the lady.

The counsellor started praising the school campus saying that it has a palatial building and opulent campus after which she gave us a form to fill.

'Sir, please mention your contact numbers and email ID on the next page and signatures here. We have a 40% expatriate community and some foreign teachers. And, if you make an advance payment for the first quarter school fee, I can reserve a seat right now.'

Wow! They were so desperate to give admission to foreign students, I thought.

'Okay, we need time to think,' my dad emphasised.

'In that case sir, leave your contact number on this form please,' she pleaded.

Yeah of course, so that you can disturb us by calling us, day in and day out to take admission in this esteemed school?

My inner turmoil increased. There was technically nothing wrong with that school. But somewhere, it just didn't click with us.

Good riddance! Mahesh started the engine as soon as he saw us coming towards the car. My dad's phone rang. It was Mr Suri. He wanted to check about the school thing. Dad informed him that we didn't like the school much.

'So, what next dad?' I took a sip of my water.

'Springfield,' he announced.

'Oh, Mr Suri is there, right?'

'Yeah, let's go.'

It is the same school Samar attends. It took us some time to reach.

Soon after, Mahesh pulled outside a U-shaped parking lot in front of a four-storey building. There was a lawn bordering a road, and it read 'Drop off zone'. I removed my earphones and put them inside my sling bag as I stepped out of the car.

The security guard asked us to write an entry in the register. He gave us two visitor ID cards and directed us towards the lobby. As we entered the hall, we spotted Suri uncle. He was on a call with someone, but he still managed to smile at us and shook hands with dad. We sat on a grey coloured soft, comfy couch. I observed the depths of the space. The school office had four rooms in each corner; all rooms with glass doors. On one door, the nameplate said, "School Principal" and her name "Shobha Mukherjee".

The other two rooms were interview and meeting rooms. There were palm trees and other indoor plants nicely sprucing up space. In the centre, there was a reception desk. Lilies decked up the marble slab. The housekeeping boy was seen mopping the floor frequently. There was nothing made up about the place. It was calm, and everybody was professional and busy with their work. That space was so much agreeable with my thoughts.

Mr Suri finally finished with the call and told us to wait while he spoke to the lady at the reception. In a couple of minutes, we were inside the principal's office.

I liked the idea that you can meet the principal of the school directly for a reasonable chat regarding your future with their school. It was better than listening to an already-well-read-information about the school by a counsellor whose face you will only see once or twice a year when you are in the school.

'Hello! How are you, Mr Sethi?' Mrs Shobha broke the silence. She appeared very graceful.

I was guessing she must be in her early 50s. The lady wore rimless bifocal glasses. Her hair was short and wavy, with elegant white strands all over, neatly blow-dried. She wore a smart peach shirt and beige pants. As she was conversing with dad, she smiled a lot, and in between, she looked at me and acknowledged my presence. Her eyes instilled warmth. Her talks were very welcoming. She didn't sound like an austere school principal; stuffy, distant or hard-nosed. She looked modest and her demeanour was self-effacing, gracious and polite.

When she finished talking to dad, she turned towards me and asked me about my previous school, hobbies, sports interests, academics and community service projects.

After my interview, she asked her assistant Farah to show us the school campus. I was nervous and excited at the same time.

The school was a plain grey brick building. It was immaculate, with lots of green areas around. It didn't look too different or palatial. It just looked like a school. That's it! There were three hallways on the ground floor. The main hallway led to the junior classes, and the other one led to an eighty-seat cafeteria with a kitchen attached. One of the cafeteria doors led to a huge soccer field and a basketball court. There was a jungle gym corner for small children at the back of the cafeteria.

Then, Farah took us to the upper levels. I spotted a huge amphitheatre on the ground level while looking out of the design lab window on level 4.

'The view is awesome!' I exclaimed.

My dad and uncle were discussing the curriculum. Uncle suggested that IB might be a better board for me as I would learn additional languages and it would provide me with an opportunity to engage in a topic of interest with a chosen subject of my choice.

The counsellor emphasised, 'Sir, we have IGCSE as well. It is developed by the University of Cambridge and is one of the most sought after and recognised qualifications in the world.'

'I see,' acknowledged my dad.

'My son is studying here,' Mr Suri told Farah.

'Ah, okay, what's his name?'

'Samar Suri.'

'Oh! One of the brightest we have here, sir.' She showed her brightest smile too.

'Nice to meet you,' Mr Suri bid goodbye to Farah as she dropped us near the school office.

'Thank you for visiting, Jasmeet and hope to see you soon!' She handed over the school prospectus to me.

'Thank you for your time and for showing us around. See you soon.'

We strode away towards our respective cars as it had started pouring. The scooterists wore plastic covers to protect themselves from the rain, which I found a little weird. The beggars sat cooped inside the shade of the awnings till the shopkeeper shooed them away. Some were still trying to sell little knick-knacks in the rain when the cars stopped at the red signal.

Liberation is what I feel all around
There's a spring in everyone's step
There's a sudden subtle bliss everywhere
Positive vibes flowing in the breeze
With that said, I embrace what's coming next!
#Delhirains

#HouseNumberM65

Monty and I were busy with our usual banter when grandpa came to our room.

'Help me with something, if you please! Mahesh is not here, so you go to Mr Sharma's house right opposite the park and give these letters to him. The house number is M-65. Their letters keep coming to us for some reason,' he said and handed the three letters over to Monty. After that, he readjusted his glasses and left towards his room.

We decided to go together. There was nothing beautiful about the community park. The grass and the trees were yellowish-green. The leaves of the trees were coated with dust. The jogging track was not clean and there was no sign of any person at that time in the park, apart from a poor slim street dog, resting under a tree and scratching his feet once in a while.

Soon, we were standing in front of this large building with a small lawn in front. Above us, we saw a camera looking at us. The moment we rang the doorbell, we heard a dog barking from inside.

'Hello?' A girl appeared, raising her eyebrows, leaving us uncomfortable.

'Hi, I am Monty. These mails keep coming to our address by mistake.'

'Oh, gosh! Again? I have no idea why these letters keep coming to your house! I will speak to dad,' she replied coldly.

'Well, thank you very much.' Her bling phone rang, and she gave us a goodbye smile while waiting for us to go. We turned around quickly, before she could slam the gate on our faces.

'How awkward!' I groaned as we started walking back.

'If this weren't for grandad, I would never have done these kinds of things. Ever!' Monty sulked.

◆

While coming back, we spotted grandad sitting on a bench in the park with his friends and chatting. Now, the same park was bustling with laughter and physical activity.

I spotted my grandfather throwing a biscuit to the lazy dog. The dog sniffed the biscuit and devoured it in excitement. We escaped the clamour of the park and went straight towards our tranquil tree-lined lane. My mom and granny were drinking the evening masala chai in the lawn, and the aroma of cardamom and other spices filled the space. Lakshmi gave a big smile as we entered.

I put my arms around granny, 'How are you feeling now, granny?'

'I am fine now. Manju took me for a routine check-up, blood pressure and all. I am fine. Thank you, dear.' Her wrinkled white skin stretched as she smiled and she patted my cheek.

'Where were you both?' Mom asked us.

'We went to the Sharmas' place to give their mail, mom. Grandad sent us,' I replied.

'Okay, did you meet Mrs or Mr Sharma there?'

'Nah! Just their daughter,'

'Okay. Your dad called just now, and we are all going out for dinner tonight with the Suris. Let's not be late. So, get ready on time.'

I went to my room upstairs, took off my sketchers and grabbed a glass of water. I sat down on my bed and started checking my phone for any messages or calls. There were a couple of WhatsApp messages from my friends in Canary Wharf. We had created a group on WhatsApp for classmates by the name of "Rockwell peeps".

There was a knock at my door, and mom entered holding a platter with two apples and a knife. She sat beside me.

'Did you like that school you visited, Jessi?' she asked me while giving me a slice of apple.

'Mom, it looks nice, but I miss Rockwell. I have no clue how it's going to be,' I disclosed my inner fears to mom.

'Don't freak out Jessi. You'll be fine. Change is the way of life, and it brings new colours with it. Enjoy life as it comes. My dad was in the army. Do you know how many schools we have changed? You have no idea, darling! Change is good. You meet different people from all walks of life. Our lives should not be devoid of new things and experiences.'

Her words were very encouraging. 'Thanks mum!' I hugged her.

#TheHautMondeFamily

There was an air of uncertainty among adults on whether we should go to the Taj or the Hyatt hotel. Finally, Taj was decided on.

Well, it was quite interesting to watch adults behave like teenagers sometimes. I smiled at the thought. Being born and raised in a #HautMondeFamily, it made me wonder.

My mom and Suri aunty are the two most well-dressed women I have ever seen: no dearth of designer clothes and handbags. The hair and make-up are always done tastefully. They exhibit mannerisms of a high-class society that goes back to their family backgrounds. Suri aunty's dad is a hotelier in Dubai and they are one of the wealthiest families around.

Both my grandfathers are from army backgrounds. They have passed on the sophistication, courtesy, decorum, etiquette and seemliness urbanity to their future generations.

Sometimes I felt that these traits were present with me! And at other times, I felt that it was the gene we missed.

When we reached the hotel, I spotted Samar attending a call on his phone, looking well-groomed as ever. As soon as he saw us, he said goodbye to the caller and shook hands with my dad. He was wearing a close-fitted Ralph shirt and designer denims. His sharp facial features were highlighted even more in the glitzy chandeliers of the hotel lobby. Soon, we all joined uncle and aunty on the table and ordered some delicious food.

The adults ordered wine, and we all enjoyed mojitos and ginger ale. The grown-up ladies and gentlemen on our table were discussing how to spend their Sunday at the city club.

Wow! My social life had suddenly become so happening. In London, all we used to do were long walks with mom and Monty or just grocery shopping or typically staying at home watching movies or playing Jenga with family when it was too cold to go out. Only when it was sunny and pleasant, we would spend the whole day outdoors. From long walks to fancy dinners! It's all a little weird sometimes! I thought.

'Hey, you play basketball?' Samar asked Monty while picking up a bite of his gluten-free eggless Raspberry Tiramisu with a fork.

'Yeah, but I need to figure out how to get out of my "lazy boy" mode in the evenings.' We all cracked up at him.

'I go to this Omnia Basketball Academy twice a week if you want to join in?' Samar suggested, putting the bite in his mouth finally. I guess he never speaks while he is eating or never eats while he is speaking, whichever is earlier. On the contrary, Monty and I always like to talk when our mouths are full. Yeah, I know I told you we belong to a haut monde family, but lest you forget, I also said to you that this is the gene Monty and I missed!

I had ordered my Banoffee Pie that I relished with extreme mannerism.

'Hey, Samar, any Jazz music instructors around? I used to learn Jazz dance in London,' I asked Samar as soon as I finished my dessert.

'Not sure about Jazz but in M-main, there's a Dance Academy, and they teach Zumba and other dance forms. You can check out there.'

'Okay, sure,' I was taking another bite of my pie when he interrupted.

'Oh wait, I know a place called Bollywood Rhythms in Panchsheel Park if you are fond of Bollywood dance style,' he added.

'I wouldn't mind going that far, but Bollywood dance is not something I am looking for. I find it weird, and I just love Jazz,' I said.

'It's interesting that you are following what you like, Jess. Someday, I want to learn rhythm and Broadway tap dance too, but I have too many sports at hand,' he smiled slightly, opening his thin lips and showing his perfect teeth.Then, he excused himself when his phone rang.

Samar is so damn good looking. I wonder how many girls might have a crush on him in school and the neighbourhood. He is a dream boyfriend for any girl.

My reverie was interrupted by the adults who were ready to leave. We left the hotel but Samar's thoughts didn't leave my mind.

◆

The next day was very exciting as we were all set to go to the community club. A beautiful day awaited us.

When we reached the club, we headed straight towards the pool. The water was warm and pleasant. Some teen boys and girls were playing Marco Polo in the pool.

'It's so lame,' I mumbled to Monty and Samar.

'What do you mean?' Monty looked at my face with a puzzled expression.

'I mean it's a no brainer.' I laughed at the petty game.

'Chill girl, you don't need brains to have some fun,' Samar giggled and splashed some water on Monty and me, which started our mini splash game.

'We like this game better,' Monty said and we all laughed out loud.

'Let me return the favour,' Samar splashed more water on Monty.

When we had had enough of water-therapy, we decided to sunbathe by the pool-side. I spread my towel on the wooden sun chair and lay down, then took out my glares and Dan Brown's *Inferno* from my bag.

'What are you reading, Jess?' Samar asked.

I showed him the book cover.

'I am a sucker for thrillers.' I smiled at Samar's remark.

The waiter got a couple of colourful tropical mocktails with some fancy straw umbrellas.

'So, what do you read?' I asked Samar while sipping my drink.

'I like science fiction usually. But right now, I am reading *The Hunger Games*. I love it!'

'What kind of books do you read, Monty?' Samar turned towards Monty, sipping his drink.

'I like to read Percy Jackson and some comics, sometimes. I mean, any comics I can get my hands on. He grinned.

We all talked for a little more and drank more sugary drinks. There was so much to catch up on. We talked about our schools, our friends, the latest mobile apps, games; the list was long.

After a while, Monty and Samar went to level 1 of the clubhouse to play snooker, while I decided to read for some more time. The adults, as I could see from the glass doors, were playing poker inside the clubhouse.

We had a hearty and fulfilling lunch at the club restaurant and then the ladies went to level 4 to check out some exhibition of hand-made goods. It was a charity sale. Mrs Suri, I heard, is always doing some charity meetings, high teas and luncheons. #ClassyLadiesOfDelhi.

We headed back towards our cosy homes after a long day well spent at the club.

#MixedFeelings

Monday 7:30 a.m.

My first ever solo morning run after a long time!

I laced up my shoes. I decided to look one last time in the mirror before going out. Asics tank top and three-fourth length running tights that I got from Decathlon were fair enough for the hot Delhi weather. I tied my hair back in a neat ponytail, wore my Fitbit and went to the kitchen for my sipper. I realised my Fitbit had been reminding me about my overly abused sleeping hours, and I was not able to move and achieve my goals.

'Good morning granny.' I found my grandmother getting some water from the kitchen for the tulsi plant.

She just smiled at me while mumbling her *mantras*. I could only see her lips moving but couldn't understand a word. I filled up my sipper, put on my Bowers and Wilkins and let Adam Levine playlist rule the rest of my morning.

I waved to mom and dad who were sitting in the lawn and having their morning masala chai. Then, I went out for my run. The tree-lined lanes looked beautiful in the morning sun. It was not as hot as I thought. My veins badly needed that warm, dusty but jaunty air and the sun.

I ran around the neighbourhood park. I didn't want to go inside the park for obvious reasons. I saw my grandfather doing some meditation inside the park. I ran past the park, the neighbourhood gym, a florist and another small community park. I ran for three kilometres and then took off my headphones for a short break.

'Hey, morning!' A voice called me from behind. I turned and found Samar smiling.

'Hey, Samar! Morning!' I was still huffing. The OLED screen on my sports watch told me 250 more to go.

'So, what does it say?' Samar pointed out my Fitbit.

'Oh, nothing! This just keeps reminding me to achieve ten-thousand steps in a day, and I guess it is going to be impossible today. I am already tired!' I chuckled.

'Oh, that's a shame.' He chuckled along.

'And I am sure you are always over-achieving your fitness goals because you are so fit!'

He smiled at the compliment and then said, 'Not always, I keep trying different things. I use the gym most of the time. I play sports in the evenings and of course at school too, and they made me the sports captain for this academic year.'

'Wow! That's so cool. Do you use that neighbourhood gym called Fitness Thirst or something?' I inquired.

'Yeah, it's the best in town, and my dad has a premium gold membership that I use leisurely.' He winked at me.

Oh my god! Did he just wink at me? Can't believe my luck! #BenefitsOfComplimentingYourCrush.

'That's nice, the gym looks posh.' I tried to come back to my senses.

'Oh! By the way Jess, would you like to check out that Jazz, Zumba or whatever-you-wanna-do dance academy? It is just nearby.'

He put his right hand on his waist and tilted his head to one side. I could see his sweat glistering his forehead in the morning sunshine.

'You mean, right now?'

'Yeah, right now!' Samar said, bustling with energy

'Okay, let's go then. If it is not far, then I am fine,' I said. My eyes gleamed with excitement.

He checked the time on his G-Shock and we started walking. Soon, we were at the M-main. As we reached the gate of the academy building, he got a call on his cellphone.

'Um, hey listen, I've got a call to attend. You take this elevator and go upstairs to check your stuff. I will wait for you on the patio,' Samar said.

'Yeah, fine. No worries! I will be back soon.' Then, I pressed one on the elevator as directed by the reception lady.

When the elevator door opened, I could hear the music from one of the dance rooms. The lady at the desk gave me all the details and handed me a flyer. I took a sneak-peak in one of the dance rooms since the instructors were busy.

Nice! Looks interesting! I thought.

I pressed the G button on the elevator. Samar took off his Apple airpods and inquired quickly. 'Hey, did you find something?'

'They gave me this flyer. It has some details. They don't have any jazz as of now, but they are going to introduce it in the next quarter. Till then, I can try some Latin dance form.'

'Yeah, I think you should start with Zumba to keep your bones moving,' Samar suggested.

'I hope so. Time to go home now.' I looked at my watch.

'Yeah, sure! But before that, let me treat you with the best gelato in town. I am starrrrrrrving!' He drawled his words and it made me swoon.

#NaggingRelatives

8:40 a.m.

After I returned from my eventful walk, I informed my parents about the dance academy. They were pretty happy about it and encouraged me to experiment. Just when we were about to have breakfast, my grandma's phone rang. It looked like aunt Barkha was on the other line because suddenly mom seemed to be interested in the conversation while she was clearing up the table.

'Yes, I am fine honey, just finished my breakfast! You say, how are things at your end?' Granny said with a big smile.

'Yeah, he is fine too. He just left the house with Monty,' she was talking about dad.

'Oh, then you should come over. Manju is here. You should meet her. She would feel nice.'

'What? Mum, you know what is this day going to turn out now?' I whispered to mom while we helped Lakshmi clear the table.

'Shh! Jessi, behave yourself! She's your aunt, baby.' Mom replied.

I don't know about my mom, but seriously, I have a significant issue coping with relatives here in Delhi; especially aunt Barkha. I mean, I have no problems with her coming to our house till the time she minds her own business. Aunt Barkha doesn't know what her children are up to, but loves to find out what we are doing. She pokes her nose into everything that's happening in our house. She always has this list of complaints ready with her.

Why Monty gets up late in the mornings?

Why does Jessi go alone to the market?

Why doesn't Monty sit with us and talk?

Why doesn't Jessi eat fried Aubergines?

Why do the kids use too much iPads? Not good!

Why do they like ice-cream and not our desi kulfi? You haven't taught them our Indian culture, Bhabhi…blah blah blah!

And then, she's got these two twin boys Monty's age who are always into some mischief or the other. Last summer, when we came here for vacation, they went to our terrace and filled up the water tank with all sorts of trash. Another time, they spray-painted our BMW's upholstered seats, and aunt Barkha's typical reply was, 'Oh, they have learnt this new painting technique in the summer camp, you see.'

My grandad was upset at that time. Nobody else bothered to say anything. I am not sure what they'll be up to this time. I sincerely hope Monty is back from school before they arrive. At times like this, he is my real saviour.

◆

1:30 p.m. Aunt Barkha's Arrival

My mom speaks politely with everyone. She is pretty graceful.

'Hello didi, how are you doing?' My mom greeted my aunt with her elegant smile.

'How are you, Manju? You have lost so much weight since the last time I saw you. Are you on an Atkins diet or what? Tell me about your secret diet plan.' Then she gave out a loud monstrous laugh.

'No didi, no dieting. I just do my yoga every day at home.'

'OMG! We also do yoga. I too got #BabaRamdev DVD at home, but you must be watching Shilpa Shetty's yoga DVD, right?' And again another monstrous laugh from her side.

As she said that, her twins got out of their shiny silver Benz GLA. They looked like predators looking for their prey in the wild. They went straight to the television room and asked for the Xbox. Lakshmi had to leave all her work to attend to their demands, while aunt Barkha leisurely sat on the couch.

'Mummy, ever since your daughter-in-law returned from London, you have forgotten your daughter!' she groaned.

My granny knew her daughter very well. She only replied, 'It's nothing like that Barkha.'

'Nobody calls me and invites me to their house. I am the eldest in this house; everyone should remember this,' she said while looking at mom.

'Didi, ever since we came, we are tied up with one thing or the other. School admissions are going on.' Mom tried to explain to her, but she was more on her face than ever.

I was in the adjoining room playing candy crush on my phone. Listening to all that made me sick. I went upstairs to my room when I heard strange noises coming from Monty's room. I tip-toed to see what was happening and couldn't believe my eyes. The twins had jumbled up cables of the Xbox, Tata Sky and Monty's woofers all together across his room and to each other's legs. I guess they were playing cops and robbers or something because one of them disguised himself as a thief and the police officer tied up his legs with cable wires.

This is a nuisance! I thought to myself and went back to my room to lie down for a while. God save Monty's space.

◆

Mom woke me up and requested me to come down for lunch.

'Mom, I am not hungry.'

'Jessi, didi is waiting for you, and I want you at the dining table in two minutes.'

'Okay mom!' I yawned, then washed my face, brushed my hair and went down for lunch.

Aunt Barkha scanned me from head to toe as I sat opposite to her at the dining table.

'Sleeping?' She sarcastically smiled at me while chewing a cucumber cube.

'No, I was just reading a book,' I purposefully lied, not because I was afraid to tell the truth, but because I didn't want to hear a lecture on sleeping during odd hours.

'Where's Monty, did he call when he is getiing back?' I tried to change the topic, and more than that, I was severely missing him.

'Yeah, he will take some more time. He is buying his books and uniform. We have finalised a school for them,' mom replied while serving okra on my plate.

I made the grumpiest face but thinking about the repercussions of not eating the same, I made a truce with the vegetable. Aunt Barkha had the shock of her life when she found the vegetable disappearing slowly from my plate. She raised her eyebrows and then scrunched it, but didn't say a word. I gave her a finale smile when I finished my lunch, but my aunt turned her face to the other side.

I seriously don't understand why some people scan each other's plates and measure what and how much the other person is eating? Especially these grown-ups! I mean, why do they even care, how much the kids are eating? How much is the daughter-in-law eating? If she is eating a full meal, then how come she is losing so much weight? These things are for teenagers, right? I would not lie, but I do scan Monty's portion of food most of the time. Whenever we sit and eat a pizza, I eye the next best slice much before he does. Now, I can't believe grown-ups are doing the same, and I don't see any kind of learning in it. Seriously man!

By the way, I forgot to tell you, her twins are having pepperoni pizza upstairs! Not fair!

While clearing up the dining table, I whispered in mom's ear, 'Mom, is it gonna be a whole day affair?'

'Jessi, mind your words baby,' she whispered back, putting the dishes in the dishwasher.

'It's her house first, and she can stay here as long as she likes,' she continued.

'Oh come on mom, at least you don't talk like that. She is just a normal guest. That's it! And according to your logic, aunt Barkha's house is her sister-in-law's house first, and your house is not this house, but aunt Barkha's house first? I don't get that weird logic,' I tried to reason with mom.

'You are right Jessi. No matter how educated we become, we are still slaves to certain norms of the society.'

'Oh, give me a break mom, these damn norms are too lame!'

'Yeah, sometimes I get tired too, but there is another way to see this life. Life mirrors your every thought, so keep your thoughts positive as much as you can, and life will bring you only good experiences.'

◆

6:30 p.m.

To straighten the jumbled up wires in Monty's room was too much for us. Monty got a near heart attack when he saw his room in shambles.

'Those monkeys have turned my room into a mortal combat battlefield!' He sulked while arranging everything.

'Yeah, it is like pulling a rabbit out of a hat, I swear!' I gritted my teeth in anger.

'Mom, I beg for a macaroni and cheese, please. I need to cope up with all this,' Monty shrieked from his room.

It was too much work for both of us. I got up and patted Monty's back and went downstairs to take a break from cleaning.

#FirstDayAtSchool

So, the D-day arrived. Monty and I dressed in our school uniforms. It was a grey pleated skirt for me, a white shirt, a red tie on which Springfield International School (SFIS) was embroidered with yellow thread, white socks with grey stripes and black plimsolls. I packed my bag with only three books that I got, a pen and a pencil.

I know you must be wondering, why a pencil? I doodle whenever I get worked up. I love to sketch my feelings.

My granny was watching me all the while I was dressing up and getting freaked out about this whole first-day-at-school thing! She could sense that I was a little perturbed.

'Why are you rubbing your eyes, Jessi?' my granny asked me.

'I don't know granny, just my left eye is twitching a bit.'

The fact is that I was getting more on edge about the first day of school. I wanted that day to be over as soon as possible and come back to my comfy chair, books and music. I was hoping to make some new friends, though.

'All the best to both of you!' Mom hugged us and finally Monty and I smiled.

There is so much drama in Punjabi families, I tell you, and it doesn't matter whether you live in London or Delhi! Feeding sugary curd before we leave for something for the first time is one such ritual. Monty and I thought we were leaving for a battlefield.

Thank god she did not put a *tilak* after getting inspired from Karan Johar movies! Yeah! I know who Karan Johar is! All *desis* in London watch all his movies.

Soon we were driven away by Mahesh to Springfield International Battlefield. Monty and I ciao-ed and headed towards our respective home rooms.

The hallways were busy with students walking with books in their hands. The locker doors opened and closed, and some girls gossiped and giggled in the corner while looking at me. I was perplexed.

Who knows, they might be judging me for reasons unknown to me!

I could hear two girls standing next to my locker gossiping about another girl in their class. One of them said, 'But she can't be in our gang, because she has terrible bushy eyebrows. You can't even call them eyebrows. She will put our popularity quotient down in the school! She is a big NO!'

The other girl said, 'Yeah, you are right, Belinda. What about Jasmine? She is beautiful like us?'

I was smiling at their conversation while taking out my books.

The other girl immediately said, 'No way! Jasmine can't be in our gang, she has long hair.'

'Now what is wrong with long hair?' The first girl scoffed.

'You don't understand. She got *long hair*. That means the girl has options! She can tie her hair on Monday, leave them open on Tuesday and curl them on Wednesday. I have short and wavy hair, and not much can be done, so she is a complete NO! We really can't have her in our gang. Let's try to get Yana.'

'No, she is too posh and elitist. Won't work with us. We better have the upper hand in things. You know what I mean.' She winked.

And the conversation went on. I finally closed my locker door firmly and smiled at them and got a smirk in return from them, after which I headed towards my home room.

◆

The classroom was big and spacious, and huge windows made the sunlight welcome in our class. The home room teacher introduced herself.

'Hello, class! I am Mrs Nayanthara, your home room teacher and I see a lot of new students in the class today.'

And she kept the pile of notebooks on her desk. She had long curly hair and wore a pleasant smile. She began scanning the room.

'Okay, before we start, can we please have a brief new student orientation today? For that, I would like to hear from each one of you here, new or old. Let's start with your introductions first. Whatever you want to tell about yourself, I am all ears!'

Then, she gave a big smile to the class.

'We will start with you.' She pointed out to the boy sitting on the first bench. I was on the fourth bench. Thank goodness, I had time to adjust to all that.

'Hey peeps, my name is Terrance Alves and me...'

Mrs Nayanthara's eyebrows shot up, and her smile vanished. She scrunched her eyes and Terrance seemed to notice that, because in the next moment, he was correcting himself.

'Uh...Sorry. Hello everyone. My name is Terrance Alves, and I am from Mumbai. This is my first academic year with SFIS Delhi, and I am excited...uh, to... make new friends.'

Mrs Nayanthara's eyes shot up again, and then Terrance continued.

'I mean, I am looking forward to a wonderful learning experience here. Thank you!'

I could hear somebody giggling at the back.

My hand was on my chin, and I listened to everyone, as they introduced themselves one after another.

When I introduced myself, I was short and crisp.

'Hi, this is Jasmeet Sethi, and we just moved to Delhi from London. I am looking forward to a wonderful learning experience here at SFIS.'

Terrance would have sued me for plagiarism. But seriously, I didn't know what else to say and how much introduction is a good introduction.

Honestly, what more can I talk about myself and how much people would be interested in listening to me? Would they like to listen to my stuff like – "What a moron I am at times and I get so worked up with changes in life and with new things... I never had a steady boyfriend." I don't know if the class would be interested in knowing that.

Maybe I can tell them that I always like to be in my bubble, reading and listening to music, but then I thought, not a good idea at all!

And so, the introductions were almost over when the classroom door opened and Samar entered the class with a girl.

'I am sorry, we are late ma'am. The bus broke down!'

'Oh? Which route?' Mrs Nayanthara removed her spectacles and started walking towards the door.

'Number 9,' Samar sat on the last bench with the girl.

'Oh! So the students were on the road or something?'

'Yes, ma'am, for a minute or so. And then, somebody called the transport department, and they sent another bus quickly.'

'Okay, I will be back in a minute. I will get an update from the transport and then raise this issue.'

I looked behind. Samar was busy talking to the girl.

'I have seen this girl somewhere,' my mind wandered in the past tense. Where? When?

And the sequence of events ran through my mind.

Monty and I fight....

Grandad interferes in our fight...and sends us to deliver letters...

Hello! Meet Miss Snob Yana Sharma. Bingo!

'Whatever!' I was talking to myself when the girl sitting next to me noticed the same.

'Hi! Are you thinking about her?' she pointed towards Yana.

'Excuse me? Are you trying to read my mind?' I snapped back at the poor girl.

'I am sorry, but I've been noticing you ever since these guys entered the class!' She shrugged her shoulders.

'I can't believe this! There is no privacy of thoughts in this school?' I murmured and turned my face towards her. I told her that Samar is my next-door neighbour and a great friend of mine. About Yana, I told her I couldn't care less!

'Well, to tell you the truth, she is one of those mean girls we have around. The other two are in different sections.'

'Thanks for the information, but I don't wanna talk about her,' I raised my voice at her.

And the bell rang for the French class.

'Excuse me. I gotta go!' I picked up my books and went outside the class.

'By the way, my name is Imly.'

'Nice to meet you!' By the time I said that, I was already out of her sight. When I was closer to the locker rooms, I thought maybe I was getting too stroppy with her.

◆

I slid onto the second last bench next to the window in the beautiful and sunny French language classroom. The teacher had not turned up yet, and the whole class was in chaos. I decided to browse through the French book when somebody tapped me on my shoulder. It was Samar.

'Hi, what's up?' His smile was contagious.

I removed my hand from my chin and straightened my back.

'So far, so good,' I smiled a little and then, he sat right next to me. My whole face was fifty shades of pink. Yana must be in the Spanish class because everybody gets to choose between these two languages.

Ah! Good riddance! At least for a while!

Terrance joined the French class with us. He bent over Samar's shoulders and whispered 'Hey, what's the plan for the weekend, dude?'

'I can't believe this dude,' Samar said while looking at me. Then, he turned his face towards him and told him holding his collar in one hand, 'It is just Monday man, chillax!'

'Yeah, I know that. But, we still need to plan, dude!' Terrance played with his fidget spinner while he said that.

'Such a kid! Which eleventh grader gets fidget spinners to school? Give it to me!' Samar took the fidget spinner from him and started spinning.

'You know Jess, this guy wants to party all the time. He is one crazy guy.' Samar balanced the fidget spinner on his index finger.

'How do you guys know each other so well? I mean, in the home room, he said he is new and stuff.' I took the spinner from Samar's hands and started spinning.

'Yeah, we meet in the gym every day. He lives near M-Main.'

Miss Michelle Lambert, our French teacher, entered the class. She cleared her throat and gave her introduction. And we all shared our introductions again. I yawned by the time my turn came.

'Sleepy, already?' Samar whispered in my ear.

'Nope! Just this new student introduction is getting on my nerves!' I giggled slowly, and he chuckled along. I have never seen him laughing so much before.

'Okay, forget about this, let's play truth or dare!' I whispered.

'Umm! Truth,' he said.

'Okay! What is the first thing that comes to your mind about the person on your left?'

'Just give me your hand.'

'Okay,' I whispered.

'I can tell you every single day, and I don't know if you will believe me or not, but you have a face that I feel is searching for someone. It is beautiful and serene; just like a dove flying in the azure sky. It is a pleasure to watch this dove taking a flight and enjoying the wind in her wings. You don't need to search for that special one because if you look around, people are waiting for you with their promises to keep you happy and safe. Don't find someone, someone special would find you one day!'

I was a little taken aback by what he said. I never expected these words from him. He was still holding my hand and I could feel the warmth of his soft palms.

'Are you reading something like, "How to give smart answers to a girl" or something?' I smiled and released my hand.

'Truth or dare?' he said.

'Dare.'

He rolled his eyes. 'Ok, tell me, what you would do if you were the queen of England?'

'What rubbish is this?' I laughed silently.

'Shh! Answer me quickly!'

'It's a tricky question. Who asks such questions?' I giggled.

'Okay, I will change the question for you. List five disgusting or annoying habits you have.'

'I don't want to play this stupid game.' I hid my mouth with my hand while laughing.

'Shhh…I can hear some noise at the back!' Miss Lambert scanned us and then turned towards the whiteboard.

◆

The bell rang and we got a short twenty-minutes snacks break. Samar, Terrance and I went to this little coffee room on level 4. It was a tiny room with a coffee machine and cookies, board games and a guitar.

Samar picked up the guitar while I made black coffee for myself. Terrance was munching cookies while sitting on one of the tables.

'Being healthy doesn't have to be that bad, right?' He offered me the cookie packet.

'Agreed,' I said and took two cookies, and Terrance shoved the rest of the cookies in his mouth.

'It's all about balance, dudes!' Samar said while strumming the guitar.

'Now, Listen to this!' Samar smiled.

While Samar was singing *Thinking Out Loud*, Terrance jumped from the table and took my hand to dance. I was laughing so hard while he was swaying me around the little coffee room. I saw Yana entering with her two girlfriends.

'You are superb, Mr Ed Sheeran!' She gave a big smile to Samar, but didn't care to notice us.

'Well, nice company, but it's GBTC time dudes!' she gave a pursed-up smile to Terrance and me.

'Oh, shucks! We are late for the P.E. class!' Samar banged his head on the guitar.

'What is this GBTC?' Terrance inquired.

'It is short for get back to class!' Samar told Terrance while brushing his hands through his hair.

'Oh, by the way, let me first have the honour to introduce two beautiful girls here.' And then he cleared his throat to continue. 'Yana, this is Jessi and Jessi! This is Yana...and Terrance...this is Yana...and Jessi...this is Terrance...' The other two girls kept giggling.

This act surprised Yana. She obviously didn't like it. I guess she was expecting a special kind of introduction, which never happened! She thought she would get introduced as the princess of the school or something.

Terrance and Samar scurried away to the class. Yana and I were walking together, and obviously, I broke the silence.

'You know, we have met before!' I told her.

'Really? I seriously don't remember babes,' she said, batting her long eyelashes.

'My brother and I came to your house to return some of your dad's letters, remember?'

'Oh yes, I remember now. So, we are neighbours, hah?' She finally allowed herself a smile.

'Yes, we are.' I smiled.

◆

'Now students, look here! In this handout, you will see your set goals for this year. There will be 'n' number of physical activities and you all must undergo fitness tests before we start on all this. We need to check whether you are fit and healthy to participate in all the sports activities. If you have any allergies, there is a form attached, please do fill it.'

The P.E. teacher, Mr Dharmesh made some important announcements.

'I am allergic to all this discipline. Too much discipline takes a toll on my health. I am getting sick. I am going to burp big time,' Terrance said and sighed.

'Ugh! Not here, please.' I laughed.

Suddenly, somebody's phone rang in the class.

'Gone! Whoever it is.' I winked at Terrance.

'Who is that now?' Growled the teacher.

There was not a word from anyone.

I think the teacher wanted to play it cool on the first day, because he didn't say anything to anyone. He just narrowed his eyes at the class and then continued yapping about cellphone usage.

Soon, the much-awaited bell rang.

'Oh, it's home room again,' howled Terrance.

Mrs Nayanthara entered the class on time, looking perplexed like in the morning, holding her laptop on top of her pile of papers. The head boy went ahead and helped Mrs Nayanthara with her laptop.

'Oh, thank you, my dear,' she smiled at the head boy.

'Akash, can you fix this projector with my laptop, please dear? I need to show the online portal to the class.' She requested the head boy.

And then she stood right under the projector.

'So students, while Akash is fixing the screen for us, just to make sure I have your correct data for subjects that you all have chosen for this year. Imly Grover. Let's go with you first! Economics, social and cultural anthropology, Spanish as a new language and rest remains the same. Am I correct?' She read out and then looked up at Imly.

Imly acknowledged in return, 'Yes, ma'am.'

'Next, Ananya Reddy! Dear, I assume you have French as a second language, then mathematics and science and world religions as an additional new subject. Am I correct?'

Ananya, the head girl acknowledged.

'Done, ma'am,' the tall head boy announced.

'Akash and Jasmeet are the only two students in grade eleventh who chose Environmental Studies. So, you will both have to work together on Eco-projects and initiatives throughout the year. Okay?'

Mrs Nayanthara continued, 'Samar Suri, Yana Sharma, Dhruv Mehta and Kanupriya Bilani have the same set of subjects, except Yana, who chose design technology. Both Samar and Yana have global politics and mathematics as common subjects. Am I correct?'

And Mrs Nayanthara did that for the rest of the class as well.

'So children, it is good to know and mix with people of varied interests. I sincerely hope you all work together as one team, no matter what your subjects are, and together we create a great learning experience, okay? Besides, you all have some common areas of learning like theatre, music, dance, health science, robotics and visual arts.'

'When will the damn bell ring?' Terrance clenched his teeth.

'Shh!' I was trying to concentrate on what the teacher was saying about the online portal thing where we could check our daily, weekly, monthly progress, assessment results and attendance etcetera. I saw Terrance yawning and his eyes getting droopy. I elbowed him.

'Don't disturb, Jessi!. I am dreaming of Mumbai Pav bhaji.'

And suddenly, the recess bell rang.

'Let's go.' Terrance literally jumped from his chair while the teacher was still in the class.

She gave Terrance a you-are-impossible look and said, 'Okay class, enjoy your meals,' she lifted her laptop and pile of papers and went out towards the staff room.

I looked at Samar, who was chatting with Yana and Kanupriya.

'Samar will join us when he is done chatting with the girls. Let's go, Jessi. I am starving.' He begged and lifted my books.

'Okay, let's go!' I laughed.

I spotted Imly going towards the locker rooms.

'Hey, Terrance, why don't you just carry on and I can join you in a couple of minutes?'

'Okay, sure.' We high-five and I rushed towards the locker room to apologise to Imly.

Imly banged into somebody in the locker room and dropped her spectacles. I picked them up for her quickly and handed it over.

'Thank you Jasmeet.' She smiled and moved towards her locker.

'Do you want to go for lunch together?' I asked hesitatingly.

'Sure, give me a minute. I'll be back from the girl's room,' she replied.

I loved the vibes my school gave me on my very first day. There were positive people around, chatting, gossiping, laughing and smiling. Even the people you've been stroppy with smiled at you! Wow!

Imly tapped on my shoulder.

'Let's go! I will show you around,' she said excitedly.

'So, how long have you been in Springfields?' I inquired.

'As long as I can remember.' She waved to some juniors in the hallway.

'By the way, I am sorry for being a little rude to you. I seriously didn't mean to, Imly.'

'Are you serious?' She stopped in the middle of the hallway and then continued, 'Are you talking about that class thing?'

'Yeah, I thought I could have been a little...'

'Forget it, Jasmeet! I can't believe you are still thinking about that.'

'I just thought I should apologise, you know.'

'No, no, it is completely okay, Jasmeet. Because there are people here who break your confidence every time you want to try something new. Nerds who break your heart when you try to be polite. Dumpsters who don't like you for being less fashionable or something. Or losers who think if you don't have a swag, you don't have anything left in life. And fools, who think they are smarter than they actually are.'

She sighed and then continued, 'So, just forget about it for now. Let's head straight towards the dining hall.' She finally gave a big smile to me and put her arm around my shoulder. #LifeLessonsOnDay1.

◆

We went back home together with Mahesh. Mom was excited to know about the day.

Made friends like Imly.

The first school dance with Terrance in the coffee room.

The on and off smiles of the home room teacher.

The sight of laughing strangers.

And the spicy Indian lunch, that was not too bad.

#FireAndIce

We shall overcome. We shall overcome. We shall overcome, someday…ay…ay..ay…yay…yay…

I could hear the school choir near the gate that was about to get closed. The morning assembly had already started, and the security guard was about to close the gate, but Monty and I managed to sneak in. We got late that day as mom had gone for a two-day workshop in Mumbai and I had to prepare breakfast myself.

When I reached the class, I dropped my bag first and then hurried down to the assembly area. The head boy, Akash, was at the podium.

He talked about the Earth Hour and 'Wastage of electricity in Urban homes'. I stood behind Imly.

'Hey,' she winked at me.

'Hey,' I whispered and smiled at her.

'Just in time,' she whispered leaning backwards.

The head boy continued, 'So friends, switch off the lights, fans, ACs when you leave the classroom. But, only when you are the last one to leave. Don't switch off when the others are still in the class.'

And then he laughed it off, and it made everyone laugh a little too.

'He is so cool, isn't he?' Terrance elbowed me from behind.

'I agree.' I yawned.

It's a plus point to have a sense of humour when you are at the podium. You can instantly connect with the audience. I always feel nervous. Next time if I have to be at the podium for something, I will try some jokes as well.

When the head boy's presentation was over, we sang the national anthem and then dispersed. I still had some time to turn around and watch the beautiful soccer field in the morning sunlight. The sun was rising buoyantly.

I gazed at the golden heads of the people around. Then, I spotted Samar watching me while talking to the P.E. coach. He gave me a where-are-you-lost look, and I responded in a simple-nowhere-lost look! And you know what, he winked at me while smiling and continued his chat with Mr Dharmesh.

What? Of course, my cheeks flushed red. Because of the Delhi heat! Don' t overthink, okay!

◆

We all went back to the class after the assembly was over. Terrance was walking behind me and humming Sia's song "Cheap Thrills".

'Hey, it's not yet Friday night Terrance.' Imly and I giggled together.

'You always think about Friday nights or Saturday nights, right?' I turned to face him.

'Always! You know, living in Mumbai, you just get used to the nightlife,' he replied.

'So, you go out clubbing every weekend?' Imly inquired while adjusting her glasses.

'Yeah, we used to always look forward to the weekends.' He was skipping a step while climbing stairs.

'Delhi is happening too, I guess?' I picked up my bag as I entered the class to take out my notebook and a pencil to sketch before the course started.

'Yeah, Delhi is super happening. I am just exploring places with Samar nowadays. Samar knows the pulse of Delhi nightlife.'

Terrance sat right next to me while Imly sat with Kanupriya.

'Why don't you join us this weekend? You, Samar, Yana and I? I have to pay stag entry every time,' he asked hesitantly.

'Um... No, thanks for asking though. But, you guys carry on. I have to go shopping with my mom once she is back on Thursday. Then, we have some weekend family outing plans.' I smiled and took my book back from his hands before he hid his notorious face again.

'Good morning, students!' Mrs Nayanthara entered the class with her pile of books, papers and a laptop on top of that.

She moved her laptop and switched on the projector. The head boy immediately came to help her.

'Please, can someone put the blinds? Thank you, dear.' Her smile came back.

The lesson began with Robert Frost.

'We will discover beautiful poetry today. This one is called "Fire and Ice" by Robert Frost.'

And then she read it aloud from her laptop. I straightened my back and started reading the poem on the whiteboard and got lost in the beautiful words.

'Now class! Who will interpret this beautiful poem for me?' Her eyes shone in the hope of a beautiful interpretation, but then, I raised my hand. I couldn't understand everything, but I wanted to give it a try and Mrs Nayanthara gave me a heads up.

'Ma'am, I guess Mr Frost is talking about modernisation and urban insanity. He holds the view that the world will be destroyed by such elements like deforestation and industrialisation. By desire, he means our needs have increased. So we are destroying nature. Uh, I think I am wrong,' I shrugged my shoulders.

'It's all right! You tried to give a different answer. There is nothing wrong in thinking differently. Well done!'

'Anybody else wants to try?'

I slumped into my chair in embarrassment.

Akash rose from his chair and looked at me, then smiled. He repeated the first line of the poem before explaining "Some say the world will end in fire, Some say in ice."

I am sorry but I beg to differ here. "Fire" here seems to mean our heart's desires and "ice" refers to too much hatred or cold behaviour. The poet has experienced both sides of the coins himself. Too much desire kills a relationship, and too much hatred does the same.'

He sat down and smiled at me again. I gave him a thumbs up.

'I can't understand a word.' I heard Terrance say.

'Good interpretation Akash! And, nice try Jasmeet!' Mrs Nayanthara was all praises for Mr Head boy, and I got a consolation medal.

The bell rang. We headed towards the little coffee room. As usual, Terrance was hungry and started munching on a packet of chips while sitting on top of one of the two tables in the little room. He made a drumbeat on the table while humming a Taylor Swift song. Yana continued with him.

'She is in the school band too,' exclaimed Samar.

'That's great!' I replied lazily.

The other two girls who generally hang out with Yana started singing with her, just when a chorus was needed. I always have a smile on my face when I see the two girls doing their stuff; their kind of way, it is funny, you know! They look like twins, the way they do their hair and carry the same dumb expressions at all times.

And the band continued to "Shake it off Shake it off" but I decided to go out and take a stroll. So, I took my usual black coffee from the machine and waved to Samar.

'Leaving, Jess? There is still time for the next class?' Samar asked me while looking at his watch.

'Um…yeah…but I just need some air. I will see you in the P.E. class.' I said.

'Okay.' He shrugged.

I climbed down the stairs and decided to spend some time near the animal gym corner. But before that, I wanted to peep into Monty's class. I stood outside IX-D.

The classroom doors were green, with a thin strip of see-through glass on one side. I could see Monty sitting next to a stout boy, and he soon spotted me standing outside his class. He waved too and then he gave me a go-back-you-dork look. I laughed silently and went down the steps towards the soccer field.

The weather was sunny and windy at the same time. After some time, I looked at my watch and decided to return to the class.

'Five more minutes to go,' I talked to myself. Lost in my thoughts, I just missed the basketball bumping on my head. I realised I was walking right under the basket and the ball over me, it was about to land on my head, but then a hand came to rescue!

'Gosh, that was close! It could have landed on my head. I would have fainted!' I put my hand on my heart.

'Not a chance,' he said and kept thumping the ball while talking to me. Akash Rao, the tall head boy.

'You understand poetry quite well.' I told him.

'Thanks, I have been writing limericks since I was twelve.' He kept thumping the ball.

'Wow, that's awesome Akash.'

'Thanks, um… I think we should go for the P.E. class.

◆

'Okay, today we will conduct some fitness tests, as I told you yesterday.'

Our P.E. teacher, Mr Dharmesh, said as we stepped into the class. He then called out to the head girl Ananya Reddy.

'Ananya, please take this list from me. I will be in the P.E. room with our school fitness coach and health expert, Mr Shiva Reddy and Mrs Nalini. It will be your responsibility to send everyone to the room downstairs, one at a time. Okay?'

'Yes, sir!' She took the list from the teacher.

'Yana, since you are the vice-sports captain, I would request you to conduct drills with the rest of the students who are outside the P.E. room. Mr Prabhakaran is there on the field, and everyone's practising for the upcoming sports day event next month.'

'Okay, sure sir,' Yana replied.

'So all ready for the fitness tests?' Mr Dharmesh raised his voice.

'Yes, sir!' The whole class echoed in unison.

'Thank you, now proceed. Ananya and Akash, please take charge.'

Samar patted me on my shoulder. Then, he bent his face forward and asked me the reason for not hanging out with them the coming weekend.

'I told Terrance in the morning. I have some shopping plans with mom.' I pursed my lips in disappointment.

'Noooooo, you will have to come, Jess. It's gonna be fun.' He insisted as he drawled his words.

'Umm…I would have loved to join, but I already promised mom and we agreed to spend some time exploring the markets. I am sorry for this time,' I said and smiled and tilted my head on my side.

'But plans can be changed, no?' Terrance added.

'Yeah, okay. I will anyway have to wait until mom returns from Mumbai on Thursday. If there's any change in the plan, I will join you at the last minute?' I showed my broadest smile.

'Guys, can we please move, everyone has already left for the soccer ground. We have a sports drill.' Yana called out to us. She gave a jealous look to me before leaving.

'She is an attention seeker, don't bother.' Imly whispered in my ear.

'Now she is worried I am talking to the boys,' I whispered back to her.

◆

Meanwhile, two more days had passed before mom arrived from Mumbai. I found her drinking her usual masala chai with granny after I returned from my Zumba class that evening.

'Oh, I missed you mom!' I kissed her cheeks.

'Granny, please do tell her I have been a good girl all this while.' I smiled at my granny while putting my arms around my mom's neck.

'Of course, she was! She made her breakfast every day and gave me milk and my medicines before bedtime. She is a darling granddaughter,' Granny exclaimed and I saw her eyes shine for a moment.

'I better find Monty. Where are you, little monster?' I called Monty while climbing the stairs to his room.

'You seem to be in a good mood today. I am surprised!' He took out his skateboard from under his bed.

'Yeah, Zumba fills you with so much energy. Tomorrow is Eid holiday, and mom and I are going shopping. So, I am excited.' I was pumped up at the thought.

'Lucky you! My classmate stays five houses away, and he said he's going to come over. I guess we should be good with PlayStation the whole day.'

'Is it going to be a sleepover?'

'Nope. Catch you later... I am going skateboarding outside.'

◆

At night, when I had changed into a bright night suit, I slumped down on my lounge chair.

I thought about Samar. I opened my Instagram and found him online. I messaged him a "Hi" and then, started scrolling the feed.

His reply came ten minutes later. A simple "Hi!" Seriously? I sighed and messaged him again. "What's happening?"

His answer came after another fifteen minutes, though he was online. "Nothing much."

You know replies like these make me sick. Was I expecting too much? He might be chatting with other girls, who knows?

I kept my phone on the bedside table and played some Jazz music and switched off my night lamp.

#OneForSorrowTwoForFight

Friday at 9 a.m.

I woke up by the click-clack of cups and saucers in the kitchen downstairs. I picked up my phone and went down. I slid into a bar stool next to the kitchen table.

'Mom, you woke me up. Are you an alarm clock or something?' I yawned while looking at my WhatsApp. Jason and Miya of my Rockwell peeps were going for a rock concert that night.

"Wow, have fun guys!" I wrote.

I noticed, Terrance had created a new WhatsApp group for the class. It was called "Awesome Grade 11". Everyone was sending Eid greetings and cards on it.

Samar sent a video of him and Terrance doing a drill at school.

'What are you smiling at?' Mom inquired while pouring the coffee in the cups.

'This is crazy, mom! You have to see this.'

And mom leaned on to the kitchen slab to see the video, and she laughed her heart out.

'Is this Samar? Oh, dear! This is so funny. Who's the other boy in the video with him?'

'This is Terrance, mom. He is from Mumbai, and he is a happy-go-lucky guy. You have to meet him to believe me.'

'Hmmm.'

'Oh! By the way, mom, you remember grandad sending Monty and me to Sharmas' house that day?'

'Yeah, why?'

'Their daughter is in my class too!'

'Oh, I see. So you all have made a gang of sorts?'

'Sort of, mom,' I took a sip of my coffee and then continued, 'Mom, they are all hanging out today, to some cafe or mall. But I told them about our shopping plans, so…'

'Jessi, if you wanted to go out with them, you could have asked me, baby.'

'Nah, I just want to go shopping with you, mom.'

'Sounds good. We can have lunch at Mamagoto, what say?'

'Yeah, mom. I love that place.' I smiled at mom.

'Moreover, this Yana is a snob. I am not comfortable with her!'

'Aw! Don't worry! You will be okay, Jessi.'

I took a shower and got ready for breakfast. Everyone except Monty was at the dining table, and the holiday breakfast spread was ready. Lakshmi had made *idlis, dosa*, coconut dip and spicy *sambar*.

‘Remember Mom! We used to order this kind of food from Southern Spices in Malmesbury Road. I just love this food.’

‘Lakshmi has done a great job,’ mom replied.

‘Amma, your phone is ringing.’

Lakshmi passed the phone quickly to my granny while holding a steaming hot idli pan in one hand.

‘This has to be aunt Barkha!’ I whispered to mom, who was sitting next to me.

‘Shhh!’ Mom curled her lips.

‘She always calls whenever the family is sitting together for food,’ I whispered again, not being able to control myself and then I heard granny say, ‘Come Over!’

NO!

It looked like mom’s breakfast was already done as she got up to clear the table.

I was thinking about why she had to come every weekend or on every holiday to our house? Even if she comes, why does everybody have to be present, like we are some sort of attendants to the Marquess of the Sethi Mansion?

‘I can’t do this. I won’t spoil my day!’ Mom spotted me murmuring.

‘What’s wrong, Jessi?’ Mom came closer with a puzzled look on her face.

‘Is the shopping plan still on?’ I doubtfully looked at mom’s eyes.

'We can go in the evening when didi leaves?' she said while clearing the table.

'Mom, this is not done. Now I am going out with my friends!' I went upstairs to my room.

'Jessi, listen, honey,' mom called me, but I was already out of sight.

◆

I sat on my bed, picked up my phone and thought for a while before dialling Samar's number.

'Good morning Jess, please say you are coming,' his voice uplifted me in an instant, and I had a broad smile on my face. I don't know what it does to me sometimes.

'No, I am not! Whom were you chatting with last night?' I blurted it out and then immediately regretted it.

'No one, why?'

'I mean, you were busy chatting with someone? I saw you online, so just thought we could chat. But you were busy.'

'No, I was just scrolling Instagram. I had my cousins over to my place last night, so I was busy with them,' Samar said.

'Hmm! Okay, I was just saying...' I tried to hide my stupidity.

'Come over! I am missing my beautiful friend from London. Don't make excuses now.'

'Where are you guys hanging out?' I asked in a low voice.

'We are just grabbing some quick breakfast at Pancakes Inc. in M-main. Just walk for five minutes, and you will be here. We have some plans for the day.'

'Come quickly, Jessi. We are missing you here,' I heard Terrance grabbing Samar's handset.

'Alright! I will be there in ten.'

I called up Imly after that.

'Hi Imly, this is Jessi. What's up?'

'Hello, good morning Jessi. I am good, tell me.'

'Okay, so we are all hanging out. I mean Terrance, me, Samar and Yana. So I thought if you could also join us?'

'Like, right now? It's going to take a while, Jessi. I live a little far, and right now, I have to be with mom; she is running some errands, but I can be free in two hours. Where are you guys meeting, by the way?'

'Actually, I don't know myself. My plan with mom got cancelled, and I am desperate to hang out now because I can't tolerate some guests coming today. I will text you in thirty minutes or so. Will that be okay?'

'Yeah, perfect! Let me know the place. Dad will drop me there,' she sounded excited too!

'Okay, see you then. Bye.'

I didn't tell Samar that I invited Imly to hang out with us. I thought they would be okay with it.

◆

When I met them in Pancakes inc, they were laughing and chatting. Yana was nice to me, and we exchanged pecks on the cheeks.

'You are looking great!' Samar complimented me, and I was tickled pink. On the other hand, Yana turned green with envy!

'Well, I think we are done with breakfast, so what's the plan for the day?' She quickly tried to change the focus before Samar or Terrance showered me with more compliments than she could handle.

'Bowl Out is a good option, I guess,' Samar suggested.

'You are up for some bowling, Yan?' Samar asked Yana.

'Yeah, of course, should be fun.' Yana twirled her hair.

'Don't worry! I will treat you with some best cinnamon rolls at Cinnabon,' Samar told Yana.

'Okay.' And, finally, I saw a smile on her face when she said that.

By that time, I texted Imly on *WhatsApp*.

Jasmeet: *Hey!*
Imly: *Hi Jessi.*
Jasmeet: *So, we are going to "Bowl Out" in Vasant Kunj & then will hang out in the mall for some time. What time will you be free?*
Imly: *I will be free in sum time...Um, which mall?*
Jasmeet: *Okay, will text you soon. Let me ask :-)*
Imly: *k*

'Hey Terrance, what is the name of the mall we are going to?' I asked him as I sat in Samar's car.

'It's called Seasons Mall.' Terrance made himself busy with the music system in the front seat.

'Let's go!' Samar opened the driver seat door and adjusted his car's rear view mirrors. Terrance was our DJ. He shuffled the songs and we enjoyed the ride.

When we reached the mall, we did back-to-back bowling and some ice-skating. We had so much fun holding hands and skating so fast at one point in time. Yana was the first one to give up.

'I am boiling now!' Yana cleansed her face with sweat wipes.

'Yeah, we know that you are hot!' Terrance cracked up on Yana.

'Just shut up, I am thirsty. Let's sit somewhere!' She moved towards Samar.

'Okay, The Coffee Bean and Tea Leaf, baby?' Samar suggested.

'Yeah, okay,' Yana replied, holding Samar by his arm.

Terrance and I were walking behind. I knew then, why Terrance felt like an underdog whenever he was with them. I didn't blame him for feeling like that because I was feeling the same. I was feeling wretched, I swear!

'Are these guys dating, seriously?' I asked Terrance in a low voice.

'I guess so! Because I see them flirting on and off,' he whispered back.

'Hmm, okay!' I pursed my lips in disappointment.

'How long will this #Flirtation-ship work? What do you think, Jessi?' He questioned me.

'I dunno! I have never been in a #Flirtationship before, huh!' I rolled my eyes at him.

'Hey guys, come, we have a table here,' Yana called us.

I put my sling bag on the chair and took out my wallet. 'I'll order something for myself.'

'I'll get it, Jess. You sit,' Samar got up.

'No, it's okay. I can order, no worries! I will be back.' I stood in the queue and dialled Imly's number because the thought was worrying that she didn't know the way to that mall.

'Hey, where are you, girl?'

'Hey Jessi, I am on my way, should be another ten minutes, I guess.'

'Okay! Just call me when you reach.'

'Okay guys, I have a surprise for you all.' I couldn't hold my excitement.

'A surprise? What is it?' Terrance and Yana shouted together as they drank their frappé.

'A surprise won't be a surprise if I tell you now, isn't it?' I smiled as I sipped my drink.

'Oh, what is it, Jessi?' Terrance couldn't control his excitement anymore.

'Okay. Just relax, guys. I have invited somebody to hang out with us today,' I broadened my eyes at them.

'Jessi, is it your boyfriend or anyone from your earlier school in London?' Now it was Samar's turn to get curious. I just couldn't stop laughing.

'Okay, let's wait for Jessi's guest, okay?' Yana asked politely.

'Yeah, of course!' I smiled at her.

I looked at my watch, and my phone rang.

'Hey, you reached?' Yana, Terrance, and Samar gaped at my face.

'Yeah, I am here at the drop point outside the mall, can you come? My dad wants to meet my friends,' Imly said.

'Yeah, sure, will be there in two minutes,' I told her.

'Guys, she is here, waiting at the drop off point.'

'*She?* You mean it's a girl? Then, what are we waiting for? Let's go!' Terrance told everyone.

We all climbed down the escalators, chatting and laughing.

'What's the scene for tonight?' Terrance asked.

'We are going to Mambos Club,' Yana announced.

'Wow, I heard it's a nice place.'

'Jessi is joining too!' Samar said.

'I will have to call my mom first.' I smiled at him.

We reached the drop off point outside the mall, and it was super hot. The sunshine was in our bones. It was shockingly humid. The perspiration surfaced on our forehead, arms, and neck.

'Oh, she is there!' I pointed out to Imly standing next to her dad's scooter.

'Imly?' Terrance spotted her first, and his eyebrows shot up.

'Jessi, you called Imly?' Terrance and Yana cracked up together.

'Seriously? Did you invite Imly? What's wrong with you, girl?' Yana couldn't control her laugh.

Samar remained silent when all that happened. He took off his sunglasses, wiped his sweat and then, put them back again.

'Well, uncertainty is the mother of all grief!' Yana yawned as she started to browse her phone, ignoring what was happening around her.

'Guys, what's wrong with her? She is our classmate and my good friend.' I shrugged.

'In a week, you made her your *good friend*, huh?' Yana taunted.

'Yeah, why not? In a week, I made Terrance and you my friends too. That's why I am here!' I tried to reason out with Yana.

'Guys, just chillax,' Samar intervened finally.

'You should have asked for our opinion, Jessi! We don't generally hang out with girls like Imly. She doesn't even have a class!' Yana rolled her eyes at me.

'Never mind, Yana. Jessi is new to this culture, babes, just relax.' Samar tried to pacify her girlfriend.

'Samy, what do you mean, never mind? I mean, look at what she is wearing, man! She looks like an alien. Weirdo!' Yana argued with him.

'Shhh, she spotted us. Now she is coming here.' Terrance hinted to Yana to shut up.

'Hey guys, this is my dad and dad, these are my classmates Jasmeet, Samar, Terrance and Yana.' Imly adjusted her spectacles as she said that.

I had a polite exchange with Imly's dad and he left. I went to them and asked about the lunch plan.

'Actually, we are already done with our day now!' Yana immediately responded.

'But we can go and sit somewhere and chat?' I suggested.

'Okay, yeah, Jessi. Let's go to Vasant Vihar as decided and have our lunch,' Samar finally agreed.

'Listen, I am not sitting in the car with this weirdo, please Samar.' Yana whispered in Samar's ear, but Imly and I heard her. Samar, on the other hand, chose to ignore as much as possible.

Imly confronted Yana that very minute, ‘Listen, you snob! Even I am not interested in sitting with you; I came only because of Jessi.’

‘Hey! Don’t you dare talk to me in that tone. Nobody in the world talks to me like that, okay?’ Yana snapped back at her.

‘Hey guys…chillax!’ Samar came to the rescue while Terrance tried to look around as if he didn’t know any of us. He passed smiles at people who were staring at us, but then, he shrugged his shoulders at them as if he was not a part of all that drama.

‘Samy, I am not going anywhere with this girl, do you hear me?’ She pointed at Imly.

‘Okay! We are not going anywhere. But can you just relax first, Yana. Don’t create a scene.’ Samar put his hands on her shoulders.

‘I am not creating a scene, she is!’ She pushed away Samar’s hand from her shoulders.

‘Oh yeah?’ Imly shouted back.

‘You are sick from head to toe; you know that?’ Yana shouted back at her.

‘And you are a snob from head to toe; you know that?’ Imly snapped back at her.

‘Who needs you here?’

‘Who needs *you* in this world, Yana madam?’

‘You don’t even know how to dress up, look at yourself in the mirror first!’

‘You don’t even know how to talk to people, see yourself in the mirror right now, how disgusting you look!’

'Imly, let's go!' I held her arm and took her to one side, the moment I noticed her wet eyes.

'Yeah, I think I should go,' she said sobbingly.

'Er...Jessi, Imly, Yana, let's go...my car is here,' Samar said in hesitation.

'You go ahead Samar, I am going with Imly. I will take a cab, don't worry. This behaviour is not acceptable!' I told Samar.

'Look, I am sorry, Jessi,'

'You don't have to, Samar. Your car is here. Just go! Yana and Terrance are already inside the car. Please go and let me handle her. Trust me.'

The cars behind Samar's BMW were honking non-stop, so he had to leave.

I turned behind and found that Imly had already boarded an auto-rickshaw.

'Wait for me, Imly! I will come with you!' I tried to stop the auto.

The auto stopped and I quickly hugged Imly. She was inconsolable.

'Look, Imly. I'm sorry. I shouldn't have called you in the first place, but I never thought those guys would behave like that. I am feeling so sorry.'

'Don't be sorry, Jessi. It's not your fault. But you don't know this girl Yana. Look at the way she spoke to me today!' She wiped her spectacles with a random cloth piece from her bag.

She didn't say a word during the whole ride. Finally, the auto driver stopped at a narrow lane just outside a temple.

'Thank you Jessi, and see you at the school on Monday.'

'Sure, please take care and call me anytime.'

And so, a new type of day finally ended. I crashed on my bed at 7:30 p.m., not because I was tired physically, but drained mentally. The incidents kept playing in my mind repeatedly, and I felt worse than ever.

I checked my phone, and I was sure Samar would message me, but I was so disappointed when I saw no messages from him. He must be partying. With a sinking feeling, I dozed off to sleep, hoping for a better day tomorrow.

#WhenLoveAndHatredCollide

I woke up with the ting-ting-ting sound of the WhatsApp notifications on my phone home screen. It was 9 a.m. already. I checked my phone. I was still expecting a message or two from Samar. Maybe he messaged once he reached home last night? I double-checked my messages on WhatsApp and Snapchat. None!

Then, there were three WhatsApp messages from the Awesome Grade 11 group. Yana posted some pictures of our day out from last evening. There were five pictures, some at the skating rink and bowling and then, there were selfies of Terrance, me, Samar and Yana at the cafe and one shot at the Mambo's club where I didn't go.

Then I noticed that Imly had left the group on WhatsApp.

'Oh, man! What a day it was!' I closed my phone and tied my hair in a neat ponytail, washed my face and went to the kitchen to make some coffee. It was unusually quiet downstairs. I poured the coffee in the mug and strolled in the living room to check where everyone was.

They were all sitting in the front lawn. Mahesh was washing the car in the driveway. I didn't want to sit with the family as they would have all sorts of questions about the day before, and I was not keen to answer any of them at that moment. I sighed and decided to go back to my room instead.

I took a sip of my coffee when I saw a text notification from Samar.

Hi, I need to talk about last evening. Hope you are coming to the club today with all?

Oh, so we are going to the club? Oh yes, It was decided last week that we all would go to the city club the coming weekend.

Yeah, I am coming, I need to talk too! I typed.

I took out my towel from the cupboard and went for a shower. During and after breakfast, I noticed that none of my family members were interested in asking any questions about my outing with my friends, which was good in a way! They were too tied up with morning rituals and in getting ready for the club.

◆

When we reached the club, I spotted Samar swimming.

'Hey, want to play Marco Polo in the pool?' Samar proposed the idea as soon as he saw us.

'Nah, I will just read for a while,' I replied.

Monty jumped into the pool, and I sat on the sun chair, reading *The Fault in our Stars*.

Mom, dad, uncle and aunty sat inside the restaurant.

The air was a little humid. I missed London rains. Soon, the waiter got some nice mocktails for us. Samar and Monty came out of the pool too.

'I liked this movie, have you seen it?' Samar pointed to the book title while rubbing his head with the towel.

'No, not yet. I wanted to read the book first.' I put my book down on the table and took a sip of my drink. It was pineapple and loads of sugary syrup, but it tasted fantastic on that hot morning.

'How about a snooker game, Samar?' Monty asked.

'I just wanna sit for a while.' Samar had no clue how to initiate the talk so of course, I had to intervene.

'Monty, can you excuse us for a while? Samar and I need to talk about something.' I told him and he left.

'I don't know how to say this, but I didn't expect whatever happened yesterday,' Samar tried to pick up words.

'Same, Samar!' I snapped back and scrunched my eyebrows at him.

'Look Jessi, I know Imly shouldn't even have been there yesterday, but I ...'

'What do you mean *shouldn't have been there*, Samar?' I interrupted him angrily.

'No! I mean, she doesn't really...you know...fit in with us...and stuff,'

'Okay and how do you decide that Samar, if somebody fits in with us or not?'

He sighed and sat next to me. 'I mean, we've never hung out with her before, and I think she is a little weird,' he tensed his forehead as he said that.

'How do you decide whether somebody fits in your so-called gang? I mean, how do you decide whether a person is a misfit or a weirdo? We are all misfits, and we are all weirdos in our world. Aren't we?'

He smiled at me and looked into my eyes, as if he agreed to what I was saying.

'Yeah, we are Jess, and I never typecast anyone intentionally. Seriously, I don't have any issues with her because...'

'Because you have never interacted with her, Samar!'

'Yeah, maybe. You are right, Jess.'

'You know how bad she felt after whatever happened yesterday?'

'I know Jess! Yana went too far. I try to explain to her sometimes, but you know how she is!' And then, he shrugged.

I rolled my eyes at him.

'I don't know what to say, but Imly is a very nice girl. The very first day I met her in school, I liked her. She was very friendly to me. I was a little stroppy with her for some weird reason, but she never made me feel guilty. I felt she...'

'I understand all that Jess...'

'No Samar, let me finish! She needs a friend. I could feel it, and that's why I decided that I should call her. I know I should have told you guys before, but I just thought it would be okay. You know, it's all my mistake.'

'I am so sorry Jess, please don't feel bad. You are nowhere at fault.'

'You know Samar, at Rockwell, my earlier school in London, people do typecast Asians. So I had issues with making friends, but some of the so-called weirdos were so good with me. They were very welcoming and in a matter of a few months, I made some real friends out there. They are still in touch with me and ask about my life here. So, I just felt bad yesterday for her because I have gone through all that myself!'

'Look, Jess! I assure you. This will never happen again. You are very dear to me, and your friends are going to be my friends from now on. I promise.'

Then, he paused for a few seconds and continued, 'Listen, Imly is most welcome in our gang, and I'll speak to her on the phone and apologise to her tonight.'

'Yeah! I think you should. She will feel better.'

'Will do. Just text me her number, will call her later today.'

'Thanks Samar.'

'You don't need to thank me. Now, I will go and change for the snooker game. Monty's waiting.'

And then, he touched the tip of my nose with his index finger. Thousands of butterflies fluttered in my belly that very moment.

'Now smile! Look! It's such a beautiful day!' And he went towards the shower room.

I sighed and felt relaxed after speaking my heart out with Samar. Many times, I thought I had love-hate feelings for Samar. That day, I hated him for not showing respect towards a girl, for laughing at her and for not taking a stand! But, when he spoke to me and things were cleared, I felt there was nothing wrong with that guy.

But when he is with Yana, he is a changed guy. His wonderful traits get camouflaged by something overly possessive.

Sometimes, I wondered what it would be like to be in a relationship with him? But, what was the point in thinking about all that when I knew he was already taken!

Later that night, while lying down on my bed, I was thinking; I loved the way he touched the tip of my nose with his finger. I kept thinking about him more than a thousand times, until I dozed off to sleep.

#WhenYanaSaysSorry

Swami Vivekananda said, 'Take risks in your life! If you win, you can lead; if you lose, you can guide.'

The morning assembly started with Akash reading out the thought for the day.

It was a super sultry hot day and I was feeling a little faintish so Mrs Nayanthara asked me to sit in the class instead. I spotted Imly sitting inside the class with her head down. I walked straight towards the classroom and sat beside her. Her hair was a mess and covered her face. She lifted her head from the table and wiped her tears.

'Hey, what happened? Are you okay?' I asked her.

'Those gang of girls is picking on me every time they see me around. Everyone knows what happened on Saturday. Yana told everyone, Jessi!' And then, she sobbed a little.

'What did they say?' I asked while wiping her tearful eyes.

'They stared at me from head to toe near the locker rooms. They gathered around Yana and giggled together. Then, one of them said it aloud!

'What did they say?' I asked.

'She said...she can't stand ugly Betty.'

I raised my eyebrows in disbelief, 'She called you *ugly Betty?*'

'Jessi, they are more on my face than ever!' She sobbed again, pushing her wet glasses up her nose.

'Look Imly! This time, don't let them get away with it. You are going to complain to the principal, okay? Do you hear me?' I massaged her back so that she stopped crying.

'Imly, did you get a call back from Samar last night?' I asked her curiously.

'Yes, he tried calling me, but I just cancelled his call. I didn't want to talk to anyone. It's so embarrassing, you know.'

'Imly, look! I know that Samar is sorry for whatever happened that day. I spoke to him yesterday, and I swear he is extremely sorry.' I tried to calm her down.

The classroom door opened and Samar entered. Imly quickly wiped her nose and tears with her sleeve. I took out a wipe packet from my bag, but Samar snatched it from me and asked me to get up. He sat right next to Imly.

'Imly, wipe your face first.' He neatly pulled out a wet wipe and handed it over to Imly.

'Now, look here! Look at me, Imly,' he said and held her hands as he spoke to her.

'Samar, I know it's not your fault,' Imly wiped her tears that were refusing to stay put.

'It's everyone's fault, and I am sorry, Imly. I promise this won't happen again. Ever! I'll speak to Yana and she'll apologise to you.'

'I don't want an apology from her. I just want to be alone here. Please go.' She pleaded.

'Nope, we are not going to leave you alone like this. Imly, we need to talk to become good friends. If we don't talk, how would we know each other? And nobody is a weirdo! We are all weirdos in our little world, aren't we?'

Somebody stole my lines. I pinched him on his shoulder, and he winked.

'So get up and come with us. You are in our gang now. You are going to hang out with us from now on,' Samar announced.

Imly was about to say something when the classroom door opened and *the queen bee* appeared buzzing in her aura.

Her face froze when she found all three of us together. She was green with envy and red with anger. I tried to suppress my smile.

Meanwhile, I saw Samar still holding Imly's hands. As soon as he saw Yana, he got up and walked towards her.

Yana said, 'P.E. coach wants everyone on the field right now. 200-metre races are on!' And then she banged the classroom door so loudly as she went out that the poor table next to the door shuddered.

Samar's face went pale.Without uttering a single word, he went out of the class.

'He is so mean!' said Imly.

'Well! He is not bad. He just has two faces, you know.'

'So which one are you in love with?' And there came Imly's rapid-fire question.

'What do you mean? Let's go to the field for sports day practice and just forget about all this!' I said shyly, feeling my face flushed again.

We went out into the green soccer field, which was then used for drill practice. Terrance was holding his house flag and marching. He waved to Imly and me.

'Moron!' I told Imly, and she laughed. I loved watching her laugh. It was such a relief.

'Let me capture him with my phone camera.' I clicked a picture of him when he was about to fall on an uneven grassy patch. I immediately shared the image on our class WhatsApp group.

◆

After the classes, I went to the locker room and kept my books inside the locker. I saw Samar following me.

'Not again!' I spoke to myself.

'Hey, I just spoke to Yana and she will apologise to Imly.'

'Really? I can't believe this!' I told him.

Imly was about to leave when I called her. Yana stepped forward from her locker and pasted a sticky note with *Sorry* written on it and then she went away.

Imly finally smiled.

'Now, we are all a gang!' said Samar.

#WhenHeLikesYourIdeas

I saw the world cheering for Samar as he swam. I saw Yana and the other two girls cheering.

The two girls were shouting 'Come on, Samar! Come on, Samar!'

At one point of time, I thought they would fall into the pool if they bent any more. But the cheering didn't stop. It was unremitting. Then, there was Akash, the head boy in the lead and Ananya and Kanupriya were cheering for him. I wanted to cheer for Samar but got lost in the shouts and hails. The aura was very uplifting.

Finally, Akash won the finals!

I sat on the grass next to the animal gym corner as I watched participants for the long jump prepare. Imly sat next to me.

'Hey, you are okay?' I turned towards her, squinting my eyes as I talked to her. It was a gleaming sunny day.

'Yeah, I am okay. It's just that I am feeling a little odd. I have no desire to hang out with that Yana! But on the other hand, the rest of you all are so good, especially Samar. I don't want to be rude.'

I sighed and said, 'You know what, Imly! Stop overthinking. I am sure it's going to be okay. I think she is just insecure about Samar, that's all! She just needs Samar's attention all the time. So don't worry. She is an attention seeker. Just ignore her and enjoy yourself.' I hugged her, and she smiled.

'What's the time?' I asked Imly.

'Its half-past twelve,' Imly looked at her wrist.

'Let's move for lunch; I am starving.' I tapped Imly on her shoulders.

We spotted Terrance already sitting in the cafeteria, hogging. We filled our plates and sat right next to him.

'You're so busted, Mr Terrance,' I told him.

'Why? What happened?' He raised his eyebrows but continued eating his burger and fries.

'Oh! You didn't check your phone?' I chuckled.

'Nah, I left my phone at home, and by the way, what did you do now?' he asked curiously.

'Hey, dude, what's up with you and your drill thing, man? It was hilarious.' Samar suddenly appeared from somewhere behind him.

'What?' Terrance looked puzzled.

'Okay, I will show you, dude.' Yana opened her phone app and showed Terrance his picture and video where he was about to fall while holding the house flag.

'What the hell Jessi, you clicked this picture?' Terrance put his hands on his forehead in disbelief.

'Yeah, did you like it?' I controlled my laugh.

'Yeah, very much! It looks like somebody kicked my butt and I am about to fall face down with my dentures out of my mouth!'

But Terrance took all that in a good stride and didn't mind.

'Okay, guys, guys... I have a forty-minute environmental class right now, so will catch y'all later. I better rush.' I went straight towards the class.

◆

The room was decked up with stuff other environment students from different classes might have done for their projects. It looked lovely with all sorts of hand-made things of daily use. There was a recycled stuff corner where I saw creativity at its best. I picked up a hand-made hair comb and started to run it through my hair.

'Amused?'

I turned around and found Akash enter the class, holding a giant light bulb with a plant inside it.

'Hey, it's beautiful.' I pointed at his creation.

'Thanks, and now I want to paint the outside of this bulb. It will give an edge to this model,' he said, looking at the bulb in his hands and feeling proud.

'Why don't you put some lights inside the bulb instead of painting it and maybe hang it somewhere; it looks beautiful as it is! Just need to put some lights on.'

There was a pause for a while, and then he said, 'I think you are right. I love your idea.'

He kept the bulb carefully at the desk next to the recycled corner, and we both sat on the opposite desks to have a little chat before the teacher entered the class.

'So, you lived in the States for a long time?' I asked him first.

'Yeah! Fifteen years,' he replied with a shine in his eyes.

'Wow! So, do you like it here?'

'Yeah, kind of,' he answered.

In the hope of giving the conversation some direction, I asked, 'And your parents? What do they do?'

Suddenly, the shine from his eyes seemed to disappear at the mention of his parents.

He sighed and said, 'My mom died two years ago in a car accident.' Then, he paused for a while keeping his head down.

'I am sorry,' I felt awful.

There was a pause again, and then, he told me, 'I live with my dad here.'

'Okay, how's he coping up?'

'He is fine, Jessi. It's just that he drinks a lot, for many nights. Actually we don't talk that much, you know. I am on my own when he's at home, playing some melody on my piano. He doesn't bother much.'

I didn't say anything. I was just listening to Akash. Then, he said, 'I don't know why am I telling you all this. I am sorry, but I don't like talking about these things you know. I don't share it with anyone. I am on my own most of the time.'

'It's all right, Akash. It is okay to share and express your feelings sometimes. You can just consider me as your friend. I won't judge you.' I smiled and finally, he smiled too.

'Thanks, Jessi.'

The teacher opened the door and entered the class with a bonsai plant in her hands. Mrs Koel Nagpal smiled and introduced herself.

Then, Akash and I talked about our environmental initiatives in the past. The teacher advised the idea of re-introducing Earth Hour just for our school.

'Every year, Earth Hour is celebrated on 25 March across continents, but we just couldn't make it this time due to exams clashing. There is a strict policy. But what do you both think, can we celebrate Earth Hour in our very own special way next week?'

'Yes, ma'am! That is a great idea!' I loved the idea.

'Okay, great! So for the next two days, you both will need to work on ideas around how to celebrate this event and involve as many school students as possible.'

'But ma'am, sports day practices are on, and we just have two weeks left,' Akash said.

'My dear, the school will have events all year round, and we definitely can't put a stop on them. All we can do is to learn time management and prioritize well,' she said.

'Okay, sounds good ma'am,' Akash agreed.

She showed us the Earth Hour website and other related content that could help us prepare. She left the class and Akash and I were alone working on her laptop and looking for more ideas related to the #EarthHourEvent.

'We have to speak to the facilities to get some print outs. I'll get those after school hours,' Akash said while scrolling through google for more ideas.

'Hey, why do we need print outs? We can go paper-free. It is for the environment. We will post all the updates on the online portal and announce the same in the morning assembly for the next two days.' I shrugged my shoulders, as I suggested.

There was a pause again, and then he said, 'I always like your ideas.'

#ThatAwkwardMoment

I was a little nervous during the morning assembly, not because I haven't had my stint with public speaking before, but because I saw Terrance very close to the podium. I was hoping that he would be taking a dig at me.

I gave him a disappear-you-idiot smile at once. Samar gave me you-are-the-best-MC look.

Akash took the mic first. I was standing right next to him, pressing my knuckles with my thumb. He introduced the Earth Hour concept and then passed on the mic to me.

'Okay, umm…good morning all!'

And then, I cleared my throat and continued, 'I am Jasmeet Sethi from eleventh grade and like Akash just explained, we are specially re-introducing Earth Hour. The environment team here believes that there is no special day to save some power! It should be an everyday habit. So we thought of giving an hour off to electricity to save for our future generations. So let's switch off all power devices for one hour the day after tomorrow, from 8:30 p.m. to 9:30 p.m. Make it as special as possible; a memorable one! Make it fun, get some ideas and be creative. And don't forget to click pictures and upload them on the environment page on our online portal! The best pictures will be featured on the next year's school calendar, and the top ten pictures will be published in our monthly school magazine!'

'Woohoo! Jessi, you rock!' Terrance shouted from the class queue and Mrs Nayanthara shot him angry glances.

While we were walking back to our classes, I jokingly slapped Terrance on his cheek lightly.

'What, man!' He touched his cheek in a surprising look.

'Because you are a slap-happy guy and I love you for that. Don't ever change! Okay?' I smiled, and he looked surprised even more.

'Give me a hi-five Jessi, life is meant to be lived to the fullest. I can take some sessions for you, if you like?' And then he laughed.

'Hey Jessi,' Akash called out from behind.

'Hey,' I turned around holding my satchel.

'We don't have an environment class today, but we need to discuss a couple of things regarding the Earth Hour, if you are free?' He was holding a thick book in his hands.

'Why don't we meet in the meeting room next to the coffee room? Will that be okay with you?'

'Yeah, perfect!'

◆

When we reached the classroom for the first period, the history teacher was already in, reading something from his laptop.

I sat next to Terrance, just behind Samar and Yana.

'Vietnam was also linked to what has been called the Maritime Silk Route that brought in goods, people and ideas. French troops landed in Vietnam in 1858, and by the mid-1880s they had established a firm grip over the northern region…' And the lesson went on.

'Hey! Why are you guys in the History lesson?' I whispered to Yana and Samar.

'Actually, this particular lesson is a part of global politics, so our teacher wanted us to attend this one,' Yana whispered.

'Okay!' I whispered back.

In the midst of all this clamour and cacophony of sports timers and class bells, the sports day practices and our environmental project preparations picked up! While Akash and I were getting along well, Samar and Yana too were getting closer.

When I was waiting for Akash in the meeting room next to the little coffee room, I decided to check inside the coffee room. As I peeped inside, I found Yana and Samar kissing next to the coffee machine. Something inside me just froze until Akash called my name. I felt sick in my stomach. I stepped back quietly and went towards the meeting room.

'The management is trying to put a keyboard in that room,' Akash said while opening the meeting room door for me.

'Thank you. But who's going to play a keyboard?'

'Me!' His eyes twinkled again.

'Really? Do you play the keyboard? You are multi-talented, you know.' The kiss was still at the back of my mind, and I pretended to be excited. I just didn't feel like doing that environment thing anymore. I wanted to go home or maybe speak to Imly, but I held myself.

After Mrs Koel came and discussed a couple of more things, I left hurriedly to the locker room, hoping to find Imly. She was kneeling to her locker.

'Hey,' I patted her with my book.

'Hey Jessi, sup?' She stood holding her books.

'I had a TIA moment, you know,' I was pressing my knuckles again with my thumb.

'What? What do you mean by TIA?' she looked perplexed.

'Oh! I mean That Is Awkward moment, Imly.'

'What happened?'

'Umm! I spotted Samar kissing Yana,' I bit my fingernail. I generally don't do that, though.

'And you felt?'

'Of course…bad.' I shrugged my shoulders.

'But I don't understand why, Jessi?'

'What do you mean, why? I can't get my head around the fact that they are together!' I banged my locker door so loudly that the two boys standing next to Imly's locker got scared.

'Look, Jessi, you need to pull yourself together babes. The whole SFIS knows that they are just flirting with each other!'

'I know, right.' I sighed.

'Jessi, it is fine to feel that way. Don't try to name this feeling, okay.' Imly patted my shoulder.

'And Imly, you need to keep this little piece of trivia between both of us, okay?' I raised my index finger at her and smiled.

'Of course!' she reciprocated my smile.

#CityOfStars

Earth Hour
8:30 PM

'Sorry, but I will have to interrupt your poker game, mom and dad, because it is Earth Hour. We have to switch off all lights for the next one hour!'

'What? What are you up to now, Jessi?' mom said.

I picked up a large hat and wore it on my head.

'By the way, ladies and gentlemen, I am crowned as the new Environmental Head of the school and so we are working on this first project to save electricity. You'll have to do this for me.'

'You mean, no lights for one whole hour?' mom asked again.

'Yes, that's what I mean, my lady.'

'So what are we supposed to do?' mom was actually worried about it since it was dinner time.

'Just light a candle. And relax and chit chat in the garden outside.' I suggested.

Monty and I arranged for the mattress and chairs and a lantern in the front lawn for everyone, and then we switched off the lights.

'Your cellphone should also be off, Jessi.' My grandad's eyes are like a hawk. He spotted the cell phone light blinking from the pocket of my ripped jeans.

'Uh…yeah…sure, grandad,'

There was a message from Samar. *Hey, Jess. Come to the terrace!*

Okay, in 5. I hit the send button.

I picked up a coke zero can from the refrigerator and a torchlight from the kitchen and went straight to the terrace. Samar was making a video with his GoPro Camera.

'What are you up to?' I opened the fizzy can and took a sip.

'We have to click some pictures of this event, remember? I am just trying to take a shot of the sky and the moon. It is damn beautiful tonight, Jessi.'

'Yeah, it is. We should take a picture of ourselves; maybe a selfie?'

Our balconies are so close we could almost jump to each other's house without any hassle.

Samar and I started chatting about school. I heard a lovely Hindi movie song on the ground floor. I leaned in to check what the grown-ups were up to and they were enjoying themselves.

'Man, I tell you. These four are inseparable.' Samar took another sip of his Red Bull drink.

'Yeah, inseparable! And so are you and Yana!' I didn't move my eyes from his face because I wanted to see his reaction, even if it was dark.

There was a pause for a moment.

I poked him again, 'You both are quite a thing in the school.'

'It's not as serious as you think, Jessi.' And then, he sipped his drink and shrugged his shoulders.

'I am not thinking anything, but it shows that you are in love!'

'Hey Jessi, I am not in love or anything. I am not the kind of guy who believes in love. Seriously! We just like each other, and that's it!' And then, he ran his hands across his gorgeous hair.

'So what do you like about her?'

'I don't know, but I guess she is hot.'

I couldn't see his expressions in the dark, but I guess he was trying to smile. I smiled too and thought, *What a loser I am!*

#EarthHourEventASuccess

'Jessi, have your breakfast properly; you are just rushing to school without eating! What's up with you?'

'Mom, I am already late for school. It is crunch time, and I am not getting enough sleep due to my project and everything. I'll grab something in the cafeteria! Bye now!'

'...Vindhya Himachal, Yamuna, Ganga
Uchala Jaladhi Taranga...'

Damn! I was late again for the school Assembly!

The national anthem echoed in my ears as I crossed the torn barbed wire along with the empty fields near the school building. There were pigs basking in the muddy water in the field. Terrance had once told me about that secret way to enter the school building if we were late to the school.

I climbed the wall and jumped safely on the school side of the wall. The idea of getting caught worried me. I rubbed off the grass and other leafy stuff and mud from my knees and elbows, and scurried away to the class queue.

Before we all went back to our respective classes, Yana and I were given the task of putting up all the shortlisted pictures of Earth Hour. There were all sorts of pictures of classmates doing different things during the dark hour. That included a picture of Yana making a candle-lit dinner at home and Akash sitting next to candles, making the words 'Earth Hour' on the floor. It was a beautiful picture.

But there was an epic picture of Terrance where he covered himself with a white sheet with a hole just to see his eyes, nose and his lips. The rest of his body was covered with the sheet, and his hand was holding a candle. He really looked scary, and everyone kept laughing at that picture.

'I guess, my picture deserves to be on the school calendar, right?' Terrance asked Samar.

'No, you moron!' Samar laughed and patted him on his shoulder.

'I think Jessi's and Samar's picture looks great!' Imly winked at me. I knew she purposefully said that looking at Yana. However, Yana didn't bother to even react to that statement.

'Nobody is going back to the class now. It's sports day practice the whole day!' Samar announced just then.

'Yay!' Terrance echoed.

'You mean no lessons today?' I inquired.

'No lessons today, yeah! Saturday is sports day, my lady,' Samar said hurriedly and ushered the whole class to the field.

The drill practise was on, and Akash was holding his house flag. We exchanged smiles. After the drill practice was almost over, he sat beside me near the animal gym corner.

'So this is where I find you when you are doing nothing, right?' He put his arms on his folded knees.

'Yeah, most of the time! I prefer to read or doodle in my free time.'

'Interesting! Well, congratulations! Earth Hour was a huge success and 87% participation from school! Even the principal and rest of the school staff participated.'

'Yeah, you pulled it off really well Akash, with all your ideas and research,' I told him.

'Not without your help,' he smiled at me looking straight into my eyes and then got up roughing up his hands!

'Oh, by the way, I didn't paint the light bulb. I just put some nice plant inside it with lights. I wanted to show you, maybe tomorrow?'

'Yeah... tomorrow for sure!' I gave him a thumbs up.

#TheWrongLane

The skill events were on. There was Dhruv on the mic, 'Warm up and Stretch. Remember to warm up and stretch!'

The relay races were on. The sprinters were seen exchanging batons along the circuit.

Everyone was cheering for someone.

'Keep running!' Yana, Imly and I screamed as we saw Samar release his baton.

'Oh no! He went to the wrong lane!' I was surprised when I saw Samar on the wrong lane.

'What is he up to?' Yana was shocked.

'I've never seen Samar like this! Does he even know what he is doing?' Imly wailed.

Two sophomores sitting behind us were laughing at Samar. Yana and I turned and gave them a shut-up-you-morons look, and they all got up and sat elsewhere.

By the time Samar realised he was in the wrong circuit lane, it was too late. He was not even a runner-up. He lost!

'I am so shocked!' Yana sulked and lit out a cigarette.

'What are you doing Yana? The vice-principal is right there!' I tried to hide her cigarette with my hand.

'You want a drag?' She shrugged her shoulders.

'No, I don't smoke,' I folded my arms.We all sat down to watch the next set of skill events because after that we all had to be ready for the drill.

The drill went on really well, and we could spot our parents clapping for each house. The last part was the award ceremony. I congratulated Akash for winning the gold medal in swimming and relay race.

'Hey Terrance, did you get any medal?' Imly asked Terrance casually.

'Hehe, nope! I am such a useless guy. Tell me about the party tonight and the after-party at Samar's house.'

'I don't know about any party tonight. I just saw Samar a few minutes ago with a *firang* guy,' Yana told Terrance.

'Where is Samar now? He didn't even meet me today?' Yana was so pissed off that she lit another cigarette.

'Who is this firang guy?' Terrance inquired.

'I don't know exactly, but I heard he is Mr Montgomero's nephew. He came here for a few days from Germany,' Dhruv said as he joined to take a puff from Yana's cigarette.

'Mr Montgomero? The political science teacher?' I asked.

'Yeah! I gotta go now; my parents are here.' Dhruv left.

'Oh! What's up with Samar today?' Yana was so annoyed.

'Hey Yana, you are the vice-sports captain, so aren't you supposed to be at the podium for the award ceremony?' I asked her.

'I don't know, man! Samar is the sports captain even though he is nowhere to be seen. He's not even picking up my phone call,' Yana whined.

After the awards ceremony, I, Yana, Imly and Terrance all split up in different directions. I went home with mom, dad and Monty and took a long nap. When I got up, I had missed calls from Samar, Terrance and Imly.

I decided to call Samar first and he told me to get ready for the party; he would pick me up. I was hoping to speak with him about what happened in the drill.

◆

We went to this happening place called Tappers which is like a party place for people like us; non-alcoholic school kids. We all partied hard and danced like crazy.

'Did you see the firang guy with Samar?' Terrance pointed out towards Samar standing next to that guy.

I was not able to hear him due to the loud music so he took my hand and led me towards where they were standing.

'Hey guys, meet Gabe, Mr Montgomero's nephew!' Samar introduced him to us.

'Hi, nice to meet you Gabe,' Terrance and I then shook hands with him.

'So Gabe is short for Gabriel, I guess?' I asked him when we moved towards the open terrace to escape the loud music so we could all talk for a while.

'Yeah, Gabriel it is, and you are Jessi?' He took out a cigarette from his pocket.

'You don't look like you are in high school?' I asked him.

'Yeah, I started college this summer. Do you want a drag? Anyone?'

'No! Thanks for asking,' Terrance replied.

'No, I don't smoke. Thank you,' I replied.

Samar took a puff from him.

'So, what are you guys doing after the party?' Gabe asked.

'After-party is at my place,' Samar told him.

'Why don't you all come over to my place? It's nearby,' Gabe insisted and looked at Terrance and me.

'No, I think I can't make it. I already told my parents I would be coming on time and then, we were thinking of spending some time at Samar's place.

'Hey, I am going back next week. Why don't you guys come over? I insist,'

'Sounds good,' Samar said.

'But Samar…?'

'I will speak to your mom Jessi.'

So all of us sat in Samar's car and went to Gabe's house for the after-party.

◆

When we reached, we saw it was a beautiful house with a big lawn and a private swimming pool. The inside of the house was equally amazing with the finest of interiors from across the world.

'Wow, man! This is so cool!' Terrance seemed awestruck.

'Come on in guys. This is all yours for tonight.' Gabe ushered us in.

The lighting was dim and Gabe played some trance music on his iPod. There were comfy floor cushions and low tables and sofas. Imly, Terrance and I sat down on the floor cushions and started chatting. Yana and Samar were dancing to the music. Gabe got some beer from the kitchen and changed the track to some Jazz dance number.

'I actually wanted you guys to enjoy. That's it! Carry on!' He winked at Samar and Yana.

'Thanks!' Yana winked back at him.

Later, Yana and Samar shared a beer together. They cuddled and sat on the couch together. I could make out from Samar's expressions that he wanted to spend some time with friends rather than with Yana. Gabe sat on the arm of the couch right next to Yana to engage her in some conversation.

'I will get some beer from the kitchen,' Samar got up, leaving Yana in conversation with the lovely stranger.

I wanted to speak to Samar regarding the sports day event, and so I followed him in the kitchen.

'Hey, are you going to drive your car after this?' I pointed at the beer can.

'No way! You are going to drive. Did I tell you that?' He flashed his perfect smile and touched the tip of my nose. It was so distracting for a moment that I forgot why I was there in the kitchen following Samar.

'Dude, what was wrong with you during the race?'

'Shh! Come with me.' He took my hand and then we went to the balcony adjacent to the kitchen. It opened to a lovely view of the garden.

He said, 'Listen, Jess! Just keep this a secret between you and me, okay? Gabe gave me a very strong dose of a drug that day, and that's how I was not able to win the race. My brain became disoriented for some time.'

'What? What did you try?'

'I can't tell you that.'

'Was it weed?'

'Jess, I just wanted to try once. I swear I am not getting addicted to it. Trust me!'

Samar took a sip of his beer and we started watching the beautiful surroundings again. I broke the silence as I was worried for Samar.

'You know Samar, I've seen many of my classmates getting addicted to the stuff and then suffering in the rehabilitation centre. I just hope you don't get addicted to it. I care for you, Samar.'

'I won't do it again Jess. I promise!' And then he held my hand.

'Can I hold your hand for some time?' he asked.

'Okay!' He held my hand for some time. We quietly watched the lights.

Gazing at the gloomy skies this late I wonder as I wait.
Tomorrow will be brighter, I suppose.
Leaving behind all that I have,
Everything else but the fond memories I keep.
Sun will shine more.
Will I shine or break, only time will tell.
I will take cover in you, the lone star in my view.
Guide me and always be with me.
For you, my only trust.#Hope

19
#SavingMyFriend

Last night, Imly and I had a great sleepover. We had a lot of fun and gossiped. Not the usual girl sleepover nights which are projected in popular movies where girls have pillow fights!

It was my turn to visit Imly's house. Mahesh took us to her place. There was too much traffic on the way, so Imly and I talked about everything we did last week.

When we reached, Imly's mom welcomed me and told me that she had heard a lot about me from Imly. I exchanged greetings with her mom, dad and grandmother. I thought we would go straight to her room to chat for a while, but there was no escape from her loving family. We had to sit in the living room where her granny scanned us from head to toe with her old wrinkly eyes. Imly's mom went to the kitchen and started frying something.

'Would you like to have *lassi*?'

'Uh, no aunty! I am lactose intolerant,' I replied politely.

'What is that?' Her mom inquired, raising her eyebrows.

'Mummy, that means she is allergic to milk products,' Imly clarified.

'Oh, I understand. She is London returned, that's why?'

'NO! Mummy, just leave it here, please. Argh!' Imly took me to her room where we had fried snacks that her mom had made especially for me.

When it was time to leave, I picked up my satchel and went outside in the parking area. I couldn't find my car or Mahesh, so I called my driver, but he didn't pick up. There were so many people on the street. The street was abuzz with dogs, cows and street hawkers and the small kids were playing amidst all this.

Finally, I found him waiting for me. He drove very carefully within the crowded lanes and took me home.

For a change, I wanted to sleep with granny. But, little did I realize that her snoring would obstruct my slumber. Tossing between sleep and wakefulness, I thought of calling Samar. I thought I should tell him what he was doing wrong. Like I said, maybe he was not getting that kind of emotional support from Yana, so I thought he needed someone to talk.

I got up and went to the attached balcony to dial his number. He picked up on the first ring.

'Hey Jessi! What's up?'

'Hey, Samar! Just thinking about you.Why are you doing this?'

'Jessi stop!'

'No! You don't know what you are getting into!'

'I know everything. I am in no way getting addicted to all that. I just feel good. I feel I can do anything in this world, you know what I mean?'

'Samar, you are already good at everything you are doing. You are the sports captain, you are good in academics and you play good music. What else do you need in life? You don't need "stuff" to get high on life unnecessarily!'

'Jess! I just don't want to lose in life. I always want to win. It just gives me the feeling that I am the best.'

'But that's a fake, temporary feeling! And if you are talking about performance, what happened to that on sports day? Why didn't you win this time when every year you are the winner? Can you answer that? Because these things are temporary and will ruin you. I have seen my friends fighting with their lives in rehabs.'

'You know Jess, Yana is calling me and I have to pick up her call, please.'

'Yeah, sure!' I hung up the phone.

I went back to the room where my granny was snoring with her mouth wide open, *sans* her dentures.

Then I tried to close granny's jaw with my thumb. It was closed for a while, and the snoring stopped. I hugged her, and we slept the whole night peacefully.

#SniffSniff

'Ma'am, anything wrong, the police are here?' Akash inquired.

We were at the history class as the teacher was beginning to start the lesson on Non-Cooperation Movement. Akash's question surprised everyone, especially me.

'Umm! I don't know exactly, but they might do a random search in some of the classrooms. There's news that kids are doing substance abuse in school.'

Samar and I exchanged glances just for a couple of seconds, and then I started pressing my knuckles.

'Anyway, let's get to the making of the Non-Cooperation movement, page 106.'

Suddenly, in the middle of the lecture, our P.E. coordinator entered the class and started checking everyone's bag. I was praying in my heart, you know for whom.

I just wished he had nothing in his bag.

'All clear sir, thank you for your time.'

I exhaled and opened my eyes and saw the P.E. coordinator leave the room. The history teacher scrunched his eyes and looked really tensed. 'I don't know what is happening to kids nowadays?' The teacher went back, reading and explaining the lesson.

I kept thinking about Gabriel. He is the one who started it all.

What's going to happen now?

I shivered at the thought! I tried hard to concentrate on the lesson. Samar was sitting alone in the class in the row adjacent to mine. I went and sat right next to him when the teacher was writing something on the board.

'Hey!'

There was silence. And then, I held his hand after a minute. It was as cold as ice.

'I know.' He shrugged.

'I told you!' I pressed his hand a little.

'Shh! I don't have anything.' His eyes didn't meet mine. It still showed regret.

'Shh! It will be okay.' I rubbed his palm with my thumb, and he whispered a 'Thank you' and smiled feebly.

◆

'Hey, they took Gabe! Oh my god! I just saw it!' Yana told the class as she entered.

'Oh my god!' Terrance and Dhruv cried out.

'Nailed it!' Imly shrugged.

'That guy got drugs, man!' Dhruv said while chewing his gum.

'Mr Montgomero is in trouble now.' Terrance laughed.

'That's bad,' Akash said while clearing the table for the home room teacher, making space for her laptop and pile of notebooks.

I looked outside the glass window. I could see two uniformed men taking Gabe and putting him into the police car. Samar was standing right next to me. I could hear my heartbeat as the siren went on, and the police car left.

'I am feeling as if my brain is going to explode, Jess!' I turned around and saw Samar standing right next to me, on the verge of breaking down.

'Shh! Come with me,' I held his arm and ushered him outside the class. Luckily, no one was watching us as they were busy looking outside the window and chattering. We took the elevator to a level up to our little coffee room.

Samar drank some water and sat on the table and started crying. Tears came down his face as he failed terribly in controlling his feelings of fear and regret.

'Hey, it's okay, trust me.' I hugged him and told him to let it go.

He didn't say a word. Sometimes, we understand our friends even when we are not speaking. Silence has its secrets, and silence is the only remedy, I guess!

I kept hugging him for some time. I wanted to be lost in that moment from the chaos of this universe. I hope it was easy to love you, Samar!

#Ghosted

There was a giant sucking sound from my heart when I woke up. I felt sick in my stomach again. I called up Samar, but he didn't pick up.

Of course! It was 3 a.m. What the hell did I think I was doing?

I opened my room window a little to let the sounds of the crickets come in. I hated the silence of the dead night. But I fell asleep soon after.

I decided to skip school the next day and attended the Zumba class instead, mainly because I wanted to avoid certain things in school.

I spent the first half of my day at home; just lazing around in my pyjamas and watching *Haschak sisters* on Youtube and then, reading John Green's *Turtles All the Way Down*. I was so engrossed in the book that I forgot it was almost time for Monty to come back from school. I got up and went out of my room.

'Mahesh bhaiya, I will go along with you to pick up Monty from school.' I went outside and told the driver.

'Okay!' He just nodded.

I took a shower, changed into a nice white tee and blue jeans, and put on a light perfume. When we reached the school, it was already bus-leaving time, and everyone was outside at the bus parking area, chattering and laughing, holding their backpacks and satchels. I searched for my gang in the crowd.

I thought they must have boarded the bus. As I started to walk towards bus number 5, I heard Terrance call my name from the bus window.

'Hey, Jessi!'

'Hey, Terrance!' I finally smiled as if I had struck gold.

'Hey, come inside the bus for two minutes. Why didn't you come to school today?' Terrance ducked his head out of the bus window while he was talking to me.

'Isn't the bus leaving?' I asked, squinting my eyes as it was bright sunny.

One side of my brain told me to go inside the bus and check for Samar. Is he okay? The other side said, 'What if he is not there?'

I listened to the former one.

'Hey, Jessi, there is still time for the bus to move. Come on in,' he said, and I hopped on to the bus.

I spotted Samar and Yana occupying the last seats of the bus, holding hands.Terrance was talking uninterruped about the fun time they had that day at school, the school trip that was coming up and the boring History lecture and PE. But I guess I wasn't listening as my thoughts and eyes were stuck at the back seat of the school bus.

'You didn't even return my call?'

'You didn't even check why I called you at 3 a.m.?'

'What? Did you say something?' Terrance saw me murmuring to myself.

'Uh! Nothing,' I told him.

'By the way, any news about Gabe?' I asked him wearily.

'No, I just know they are questioning Mr Montgomery as well!' Terrance wiped the sweat on his forehead.

'Of course, they will!' I rolled my eyes.

The sound of the engine woke me up from the drama that I was watching in the back seat with open eyes.

'Okay, gotta go. I came to pick up my brother. Catch you later!'

He didn't even notice me? He didn't even raise his eyes from his girlfriend's beautiful hands.

#TheAutumnWalk

'By the way class, there's fun news for you all! The school has planned an outstation trip to Rishikesh in the first week of November. Once we are done with the Halloween party, we will prepare for the trip. The date has been finalised for the SpringFields annual music fest, which is going to be held after Halloween.

'So gear up with all the singing and musical talent, guys! Go, form your respective bands and register yourself at the music committee. The details are on the notice board.

'And last but not least, I want you guys to prepare a performance before Christmas for the Christmas party before the start of the winter holidays. You can choose theatre performance, dance form or poetry based on classic novels. You can choose Shakespeare, Jane Austen, Louisa M. Alcott. Make groups, and we will discuss more on this tomorrow. I want the names soon.'

'Everything happens in this school, except studies,' Terrance giggled, and I elbowed him.

'Akash, please distribute this circular and a consent form to all. Students, get the consent form signed by your parents if you are interested in the outstation trip. I don't want any forged signatures, okay?'

'Wow, this should be fun!' I told Terrance.

'Yay, I love Rishikesh!' Terrance exclaimed.

'Shh! Students, I know you all must be excited. Let's just have the final count by Friday, and then we will make our itinerary,' she responded to the raised clamour of the class.

Akash passed the circular to me, and I said hello to him.

'Hey, Jessi.'

'I guess they could use an online consent form and we could always do away with this sort of wasting paper.'

'I always like your ideas, Jessi.' He smiled.

I smiled back and looked closely at the circular.

'Not sure if my parents would send me for this trip.' Grunted Imly from the back seat.

'Hey, please don't say that! I am not going without you, Imly. I am going to talk to your parents today. Don't worry!'

'Yeah, you must do that Jessi, that's what friends are for.' Terrance joked.

I took the elevator down to my favourite spot; the soccer field and the animal gym. I spotted Akash playing his usual basketball while I was on my way to the soccer field.

'Careful this time!' I smiled at him.

'I will be, my lady.' He smiled broadly, looking straight into my eyes.

'Care for a walk?' I asked him.

‘Sure, there is still some time to buy for a walk, I guess.’ He looked at his watch.

I bought a biscuit packet from the canteen, and we stood next to the iron grill fence at the animal gym corner.

‘So, are you planning to join the school trip?’ I asked him while feeding the puppies.

‘Umm! I am really not sure, Jessi.’

‘Oh, you have to ask your dad, isn’t it?’ I asked.

‘I am not sure if he cares!’

‘What do you mean?’

‘Jessi, my dad is not bothered about where I go and what I do.’ He didn’t make any eye contact, just kept his eyes down at the delightfully fuzzy and humble puppies.

‘Hey, Akash, dude, long time.’ A sophomore student stopped by to have a small talk with Akash.

‘Jessi, can we take a walk to those fields out there? There are too many people here.’ He pointed out the empty space next to the school.

‘You mean those fields?’ I pointed out to those fields next to the soccer field that adjoins the school boundary wall next to the cafeteria.

‘Can you bunk your class? I don’t want to attend my Physics class,’ Akash said.

‘I think I can.’ I had a broad smile for this little adventure.

‘Can you jump that?’ He pointed towards the boundary wall.

‘Yeah, of course! I jumped that once.’ I smiled, feeling proud.

‘Seriously, Jessi?’ He cocked his head to his left.

'Yeah! Once, I was late to school, and Terrance told me this secret place to enter the campus…and so…' I shrugged.

'Whoa, atta girl! I wonder if the school folks haven't figured this way out yet.'

'Yeah, I hope they don't ever, it's just better this way.' We laughed along and crossed the wall.

Akash held my hand while I was about to jump to the other side.

'My eyes are closed, so you can jump, but I am holding your hand, don't worry.'

'Thanks for this.' I finally jumped successfully and rubbed my hands together to wipe off any dust that remained while holding the dusty wall.

Then we started walking towards the empty fields.

It was autumn, and the trees were shedding their golden leaves; not the ones that I saw in the countryside of London but the dusty versions of our own *desi* trees. They still looked beautiful, though.

'What's this tattoo on your arm?' I pointed to his biceps at the pretty looking illustration.

'My mom's initials.'

'Aww! I guess you loved her too much.'

'She was my everything, Jessi. My lifeline.'

There was a pause for a while as we walked amidst the beauty of the crunchy rust coloured and delightfully earthy autumn leaves. The rustle of the golden dried leaves was enchanting and inspirational.

'I would love to know more about you, Akash. I want to hear your poetry someday.'

'It is depressing, Jess.'

'I still want to hear.'

'Okay, someday.'

As we took a walk, he kept talking about his dad and his extended family; how his dad went into depression and alcohol after his mom died.

'But why is he depressed? You once told me, they always fought with each other and already separated?'

'I don't know exactly, but I think he regrets all of it.'

'Do you think your dad still thinks about your mom?' I asked.

'Of course, he does. He doesn't talk to anyone much, not even to me. Can you believe it?'

'What about your older brother?'

'Yeah, he is very much concerned about me. He calls me and tells me to come to the US and do my schooling there.'

'So, you want to go, Akash?'

'I am not sure. I don't wanna leave dad alone here. But, I am sick of watching him like this every day. This is no life, Jessi. You are so lucky to have your family by your side.'

My words fell short. I didn't have anything to say.

As we walked back to the school boundary wall in the autumn sun, I realised how lucky I am to have my parents and family by my side. Sometimes all it takes is to be with them and listen to each other and share each other's joys and woes.

#NotSoSpooky

Halloween Party

'It is the last day of October, and it is wonderful to see my students in so many colourful costumes today. It is that spooky time of the year again,' Principal Mrs Mukherjee was holding the assembly on Halloween.

She continued, 'I would request everyone to go to the auditorium please and celebrate Halloween time with your classmates. We have a special Halloween costume party for all of you and then yummy lunch thereafter, so enjoy the party and the music and food, but let's not forget the discipline. Tenth, eleventh and twelfth graders will go first and be free in two hours' time and attend their regular classes. No bunking of classes, please.'

'Woo!' Everyone echoed in the assembly area.

'Hey Jessi,' Imly swung her broom in the air. She was in the witch costume.

'Hey, you look cool, Imly.' I hugged her.

'But you steal the show.' She was pointing towards my wonder woman costume.

'You girls look cool, man!' Terrance appeared from somewhere. He was in a cowboy costume.

'Hey, you look cool too!' I told him.

'Let's go to the auditorium and rock it babes,' Terrance announced.

'Let's go!' We swung into action as soon as we reached the auditorium. The place was packed with students in all sorts of costumes. Yana and Samar were dancing already. Yana was a witch while Samar was dressed up as a vampire.

As we danced together, Samar winked at me, and I smiled back at him.

'Hey, Jessi, you look hot,' he whispered in my ear.

I felt a little uncomfortable when he came a little closer to me and whispered the compliment in my ear. I cleared my throat and replied, 'Uh…yeah…thanks.'

'Girls, I'll be back in a minute.' Terrance went to the podium to talk to a sophomore student who was the in-house DJ for that day. Imly was talking to a girl next to me while Dhruv danced with me.

'Hey, I think I am going to meet Samar,' I wanted to avoid Dhruv and dancing alone with him made me antsy as he was getting closer every second.

Then he again whispered in my ear, 'He is dancing with his girl. Why do you wanna interrupt? Let's dance together.'

'I guess I saw Akash, let's call him here.' There was sweat on my neck and my face flushed.

'Leave that good boy alone, Jessi. Come on! Look at me, hot girl. My wonder woman, my princess.'

I pushed his hands away as they neared my waist, 'Enough Dhruv, this is unacceptable! I don't want to dance with you. Don't touch me!' And at that time, my words were louder than the music inside the hall, and they assuredly hit his male ego or something because then his face became red with anger and revenge.

The words he spoke next broke me from inside. While picking up his Charlie Chaplin hat from the floor, he looked one last time at me before leaving and said, 'By the way, I saw you taking a walk with Akash that day, to the fields next to the school. Did he go down on you?'

'Shut up, and just get the hell out of here!' Imly told him while holding my shoulders from behind to comfort me. I froze as soon as he said that before leaving. I couldn't believe my ears.

'Well, he and his thinking sucks, Jessi! Don't worry.' Imly reassured me, but tears filled my eyes.

'I should have never left you with that asshole in the first place!' Imly held my hand and led me to the food hall next to the auditorium.

'Jessi, you should drink something, you are sweating.' Imly opened a fizzy can of sprite and gave it to me. I stood there frozen, holding the fizz can but not taking a sip.

'What's up, guys? Enjoying the party, my gang?' Samar said while opening a can of diet coke.

'What's up with you dude? I haven't seen you since this morning. I thought you are there for friends and will dance with us. We had to dance with random boys,' Imly sulked.

'Hey, I am joining you now, so what's the big deal? After food, we all will go back again inside and dance together.'

'Jessi needed you as a friend Samar, and you were dancing with Yana? Dhruv misbehaved with Jessi,' Imly grunted.

'Imly, I am fine, please,' I finally spoke.

'She is my girlfriend, man! I told you we will dance together now after food, I promise.' Samar smiled.

I kept the sprite can on the table next to me. I was feeling suffocated.

'Go, man. She is there looking for you, go fast and dance to her tunes, man! Why do you need us?' Terrance cracked some jokes on them, and that was really upsetting for Samar. But he didn't say a word.

'I am serious, man! You were glued to your girl all the time, and you talked about the gang! What gang bro?' Terrance showed all his teeth that time, and when he was about to shove the pizza slice in his mouth, Samar snatched that slice from reaching his mouth and poured the diet coke on his cowboy costume.

'What the hell, bro! I was just kidding!' Terrance finally realised that he went too overboard with his lame jokes. But Samar was not in his senses by that time, and it hit his ego. He made a fist and punched Terrance on his nose.

The students around us turned around, 'Whoa! Whoa, dudes, easy man!' One of the sophomores shouted, and two of them laughed together.

'Hey, students! I want you both in the counselling room in thirty minutes.' The counsellor came up to them and told them.

Samar gave one last look before going out of that place and told Terrance, 'Screw you!'

'Get a life dude!' Terrance replied in a low voice and went to the other side. Both parted ways.

'Language, students!' The counsellor told them.

'Could this day get any worse?' I told myself, and Imly led me to the locker area outside our classrooms.

◆

I looked at myself in the washroom mirror and then cried a bit more openly. Then, I washed my face and took out my pair of jeans and a white tee that I was carrying in my backpack to change. When I changed to my normal self, I felt a bit better, but my eyes were still red.

How can I go outside like this? I can't even talk right now? And I sobbed and sobbed.

Dhruv's words echoed in my ears and I shrieked with a pain in my heart as I sat on the bathroom floor.

There was no one around as everyone was busy at the party and classes. It was when the class bell rang, and I could hear the footsteps of girls walking and chattering, that I picked myself up and washed my face again, wiped it with a tissue and without making any eye contact with anyone, went straight towards the school office.

'I can't stay in the class anymore today.' I told myself and reported sick to the main office, asking for a leave. My mom was called, and she immediately sent the driver. I gave one last look to the hallways before I went outside to the pickup area.

◆

'Are you okay, honey?' My mom touched my forehead as soon as I reached home.

'I am okay mom, just a little tired. I am going to go upstairs and rest for a while.'

I wanted an escape from all that had happened. I slept as soon as I changed into my pyjamas. I didn't read a book, I didn't listen to any music, and I didn't lounge in my chair. I wanted the thoughts in my mind to take a break.

◆

'Jessi!' There was a faint knock at the door and I could hear mom's voice in my dreams.

'Jessi, open the door, honey!' Another set of knocks with the voice getting clearer and clearer with every single knock in my head.

I looked at the watch. It was 5:30 p.m., and the door knocks were real. Mom was outside the door, repeating my name intermittently. I opened the door to let her in.

'Are you fine, honey? You don't sleep that much during the day,' mom said in a trembling voice and touched my forehead.

'Yeah, I am okay mom, I was a bit tired.That's it.' I held the door between mom and me.

'Okay, someone has come to see you, Jessi,' she said and smiled and led the door open.

'Mom, I am in my pyjamas! Who is it?' I frowned.

'Happy Halloween, trick or treat?' Samar stood at the door behind mom, holding a pumpkin basket in his hand.

'Oh my god! Are we in kindergarten?' I laughed.

'May I come in?' he smiled. Definitely, that was an effort to make me smile. I knew it.

'Come on in,' I ushered him inside my room.

'I can't believe you are here with a pumpkin trick or treat basket, my goodness!' I sat on my bed with the pillow on my lap, and he sat on the couch next to the bed.

'Well, someone told me that the amazing Wonder Woman disappeared as she was feeling sick?' He smiled as usual.

'Um...nothing...just a ...'

'Jess, Are you okay?'

'Yeah, but what about you and Terrance?' I asked.

'What about that? He needs to keep his mouth shut.'

'Cool down, it was just a joke I guess,' I tried to pacify him.

'But he has to apologise for his behaviour. I don't appreciate anyone telling me what I need to do and whom I need to spend my time with?' Samar frowned.

'Yeah, but he just wanted you to be in the gang more because he is the only guy and he feels odd sometimes.'

'You think so, Jess? Oh, by the way, Imly was saying something when all of that happened. Um...something...she said outside the food hall. That Dhruv misbehaved with you? I mean, I was just wondering, did it really happen?'

And as he said that, tears came rolling down my cheeks like they were waiting for someone's arrival to tell their story.

'Hey, Jess... tell me what happened. I swear, I will break his head!' Samar got up immediately to comfort me.

'He didn't do anything, Samar, don't worry. But what he said about me…' I started crying again.

'What did he say to you, Jessi?' Samar got impatient.

I wiped my tears and then turned towards Samar, who was now sitting next to me, 'Samar, the other day, I bunked the class with Akash…'

'Wait! What? Did you bunk the class with Akash? What happened to your taste, man?' He cracked at me but then, made a serious face after realising that the discussion was supposed to be serious.

'So he was talking about his dad and his family, and we thought of taking a walk in those fields next to the school. And Dhruv saw us that day… and took it to another level.'

'What did he say?'

'He said bad things about Akash and me.That we were… you know what I mean. I am ashamed to even tell you what he said, Samar. I hate him for that. I fear he might gossip around in the school.'

'Idiot! What led to this kind of conversation between you and him?'

'I refused to dance with him and told him to take his hand away from my waist. He was getting too close to me at the party.'

'Jessi, I am gonna break his legs tomorrow, I swear!'

'Samar, no! You are not doing anything like that!'

'I can't promise Jessi, but I have to teach him a lesson.'

'If he doesn't say anything, please don't do anything. It will create more misery for me in school. I hope you understand,' I pleaded.

There was a pause, and then he continued, 'But Akash? I mean, he is such a strange guy. Did he bore you with his piano lessons or depressing poetry that he writes? Haha! Sorry, I just wanted you to smile.'

'He's a nice guy Samar. His life is not easy. I just want to be his friend.'

'Well, I will just suggest that you stay away from him for a while. Especially because of the gossip.'

'Hmmm...okay,' I agreed.

#MusicInTheAir

I was talking to Imly and Terrance since the home room teacher was not there when the bell rang for the music class.

'Hey, I have music. See you guys in the little coffee room after my class,' I told Imly and Terrance and went out of the class.

When I reached the music room, it was unusually quiet. A short spectacled sophomore student was sitting on a chair and adjusting the strings of his cello.

'Hi,' my voice echoed in the awkward silence of the room.

'Hi, I am William. Will, in short,' he introduced himself.

'I am Jasmeet, Jessi.' And we laughed together.

I sat down on a high wooden stool with my guitar.

'Are you in the school band too?' I asked him.

'Nope, I am not in any of these school bands. I play solo. I am preparing for the school's annual music fest myself.'

His disgruntled look said something else.

'That's awesome, why aren't you in a band or something?'

'Mainly because I can't keep up with the band members as they always have their own thing and I prefer to keep it solo.

These guys spend more time in nonsensical things. Hanging out and bullying rather than practising, so I decided I am out of all this!' He raised his hands in surrender.

'Hey, scumbag! How are you doing, man?' Two sophomores entered the music room.

'See, that's what they do to you, they bully!' Will scoffed.

'Hey littleboy! Come, let's go in the boy's room and fag,' the short guy pestered him.

'No, thank you. I don't smoke!' Will replied, keeping his eyes down on his cello.

Then, one of those boys came closer to Will. He got his face really close to him and said, 'You are such a sissy man, come on! Be a man!'

'Only sissies play the cello,' the other guy laughed.

'Stop bullying him. I will go to the counsellor if you continue!' I told them.

They rolled their eyes and left finally.

The music teacher entered the room and so did the rest of the students, including Akash, Yana, Samar, Dhruv and other senior boys and girls I didn't know.

'Hey, did you register yourself for the fest too?' I asked Akash.

'Yeah, I play keyboard. I told you that day.'

'Yeah, I remember! Someday, I want to see you play live.' I smiled broadly.

'Sure, anytime, come over to my house,' he said shyly.

'I am not sure if that is the right thing to do. You know, there are people talking behind our backs.'

'Seriously, Jessi?'

I was trying to tell him what Dhruv thought about us when Samar came right between us.

'Hey Jessi, what are you doing here? We are forming a band, come, let's decide the name and other things.'

And he gave one last look to Akash before taking my hand and leading me to the carpeted floor in one corner where Yana was sitting with her two girls, giggling of course! What else do you think they usually do?

And Samar dragged me away from Akash. I sat next to him on the carpeted floor. I said, 'Hey, you are going to play the guitar, and Yana's going to sing. What will I do?'

'You are going to sing too Jess, with your guitar. Actually, we have chosen a theme where all of us are going to sing our bits and play our own thing. Just like a jazz performance?'

'Wow, this sounds like a plan.' I was happy to be in a band.

'I have a great idea. Let's write a song sequence wherein the song itself tells a story, and we all sing our bits like Samar said, and play our respective characters and dress up like that.'

'Sounds interesting!' Yana said after taking out the pen from her mouth and smiling at Samar running her hands inside Samar's gorgeous hair.

'I got a name for our band!' I exclaimed.

'What is it?' They both echoed together.

'*The Music Story*! Do you guys like it?'

'Yeah, why not?' Samar agreed.

'Let's start working on it, guys. We have to win!' After discussions and playing some chords, the bell rang for the twenty-minute snack break.

'Are you guys going to the coffee room? I have to meet Terrance and Imly there,' I picked up my guitar as I said that.

'I don't want to talk to Terrance. Yana, let's go to the cafeteria. I am really starving. See you, Jessi.' Samar told me.

'See you, Samar,' I said and sighed.

When I reached the little coffee room, I spotted Terrance tapping on the desk and jamming with Imly.

'*The scars of your love remind me of us*

They keep me thinking that we almost had it all...'

'That's deep, dude!' I clapped.

'Hey, it's gonna be fun in Rishikesh and so excited about the fact that we are going on a road trip!' Terrance exclaimed.

We were looking forward to our trip together.

#OpenMicEvent

I could see the cheer and excitement all around the school hallways and locker. It was finally the Open Mic event!

The assembly took place inside the classrooms for everyone as the assembly area was getting revamped for the performances. There was a big banner that said, ON THE SPOT REGISTRATION.

After the assembly, we went to the locker rooms to keep our books while the event had already started. We could hear the MC announcing the event.

'...And our very first performance of the day comes from someone who's very fondly known as our school's golden girl with a golden voice. She is doing solo this time with a beautiful song that is composed by her. Boys and girls, let's hear it for Samreen Khan!'

'Hurry up Jessi, Yana. We are getting late!' Samar pleaded, but we kept giggling while combing our hair.

'There is still time, sweetheart.' Yana winked at Samar.

We all sat on the carpeted floor of the backstage, waiting for our turn; feeling nervous.

'She really sang well,' somebody said, and we agreed.

'...And now boys and girls, please welcome on stage, the poetic genius of SFIS and the winner of three national and international poetic events. Can you guys guess? Yes, our very own charming head boy Akash Rao. Please give a big round of applause for Akash!'

'Ha! *Charming head boy*! Joke of this decade!' Samar covered his lips to hide his sarcastic smile, and Yana giggled with him.

All those sleepless nights,
You spent watching me,
You lay awake holding me close
If I'd cried, you said you won't let me go
Always there, when I am taking the stairs
Holding my hand, until I enter the school's gate
Nervous I used to come, and you used to shout my name
I rejoiced to see your glorious face
Furled my passion, gave wings to fly
I felt your smile and dream to rise
A treasure lost, when I saw you leaving
We all mourn, while I couldn't stop crying
For us, it's eclipse in broad daylight
Every wall here talks about you
Your selfless deeds and kind attitude
A soul to search upon the earth
A teacher, a mother, a wife, and a friend for all
My constant in ever-changing reality,
Wish to be kind and generous as you,

On an endless road called life,
Now we all are alone and mourn your demise.

I peeked a little from the backstage curtain to get a glimpse of him.

As Akash finished his poem, the crowd was cheering, and the principal and vice-principal gave him a standing ovation. I had tears in my eyes as I knew that the poem was about his mom. I clapped hard for him. Samar was staring at me, but I continued.

We were to go next. Yana and Samar stood with me behind the curtain, and we held each other's hands together for the first time. I had at least a thousand nerves playing ping pong inside of me.

'Now hold your breath for the person who is an all-rounder in SFIS, a sportsperson, a wonderful guitarist and always ahead of everyone in the class. This time he is performing with his band – *The Music Story*. Boys and girls, introducing Yana Gupta as the lead singer, also introducing Jasmeet Sethi as the singer and guitarist and Samar Suri as the lead guitarist!'

'Woohoo!' the crowd echoed.

Samar already started playing, but the crowd didn't stop cheering and hooting. I had goosebumps on my upper arms but I smiled a lot during my performance. It turned out to be a phenomenal performance. The audience couldn't stop cheering and hooting.

'We rocked it!' We high-fivedeach other.

'I still have goosebumps.' I told them.

'Jess, you played well, girl!' Samar commended me.

We met Akash on the way to the elevator, and we all congratulated each other.

'Hey, buddy. Good show, man!' Samar shook hands with Akash.

'Hey, thanks dude, You guys rocked too!' Akash looked at me as Samar and Yana were discussing something two feet away.

'Thanks, Akash,' I responded with a smile, and he smiled back.

'Care for a walk?' Akash asked me.

'Um...actually...' I fumbled.

It was too quick a question for me at that time. Samar heard him say that, so he immediately turned towards me, 'Jess, remember we have to go to the coffee room and discuss our outstation trip?'

I had a tough situation at hand. I didn't want to let Akash go, but I guess he felt uncomfortable.

'It's okay, you guys carry on. I have some work in the lab...' Akash said in a hesitant tone.

'No, it's completely okay. Join us in the coffee room... please,' I said, trying to make him feel better.

'Yeah, come! Join us, dude,' Yana said that and that made Samar angrier, but he kept quiet, and we all went to the coffee room.

I felt bad for Akash – not because he was not welcomed by my gang but because he needed a friend, and I wanted to be his friend. But, I was confused. I hated myself for getting validation from Samar, but what happened last week also made me sick whenever I thought about it! I had mixed feelings in my mind. Nevertheless, my instinct told me to be a friend to Akash. So, I agreed to listen to my visceral brain.

'When are they going to announce the results?' Yana questioned Samar while filling her cup of lemonade from the machine.

'You mean for the open mic?'

'Yeah,' Yana said, taking a sip and grabbing a chair.

'No, actually they are not promoting competition this time. They said they only want to encourage more artists to participate,' I said.

There was a brief silence. Then, Yana broke the ice.

'So what's the plan for the Rishikesh trip?' she asked.

'You and me,' Samar returned with the chips and came closer to Yana's face.

'Guys please!' I raised my voice in disgust.

'Sorry, Jess!'

I was feeling a little awkward because of a lot of things at that time. Firstly, my buddies, Terrance and Imly were not there, and I was missing them. Secondly, the PDA of Samar and Yana was making me despicable, and thirdly, I could barely depend on Akash for a conversation because he speaks less, so I had to finally ask him, 'Care for a walk?'

'Yeah sure,' he threw my coke can into the nearby trash bin and got up.

'Let's go to the environment class. Remember, we have to finish our bottle plant project?' I reminded him.

'Yeah, as you say, Jessi.'

◆

We went into the environment class. I picked up the bottle plant project and looked at it vehemently.

'I am getting stressed out about this project.' Akash sat on the table next to the window.

'Really?' I smiled.

There was a pause for a moment. I was staring at Akash as he was putting some wet soil in the bottle.

'Hey, you know you should join us for the Rishikesh trip. I mean, I don't want you to miss out on these things in life!' I turned to face him.

'Why?' he said.

'What I mean is, you should live your life. You should make more friends'

He sighed and kept the bottle at one corner of the window and turned towards me, 'You know, Jessi, when I go back home from here, I feel sick. I miss my mom every single day and there is no one to talk to. And, when I see dad drinking, I just can't cope up. Jessi, I am dying before actual death...'

'Akash, can I come to your house today evening to speak to your dad?'

'Really? You want to do that?'

'Yeah! I mean really!'

'What are you going to talk about?'

'Permission. I will ask him if you can come to Rishikesh with us.'

I picked up my bag and left the room smiling.

Mom, you are right! Trust your instincts more than anything else.

26
#PrettyPlease

'Rishikesh?'

'Yes, sir! The whole class is going,' I hesitantly spoke to Akash's father.

'I have never stopped Aki from going anywhere! If he wants, he can go,' Mr Rao puffed his cigar and spoke.

'Okay, so it's a yes from you then?' I crossed my fingers again.

'Yes, if he wants, he can go. I have no issues.'

Akash and I were thrilled to hear this. We were trying to control our smiles. Just then, Mr Rao spoke.

'Nader, get me my drink!'

It was a signal for us to leave his space. We went upstairs to Akash's room.

'He never speaks that much with anyone!' Akash said while opening the door of his room.

'So you mean it was a good sign?' I asked while sitting on the couch in his room.

'I don't know Jessi. What will you take? Coke Zero? Red Bull?'

'I am okay, thanks.'

'Some chocolates?'

I looked at the beautiful Swiss Mountain on the wrapper of the little Lindt placed on his bedside table. 'Sure, thanks.'

'You okay, Jessi?' he asked me as I kept looking at the chocolate wrapper.

'Yeah, I am, don't worry. I am thinking about something.'

'About what?'

I sighed. 'About Terrance and Samar. They had a tiff at the Halloween party'

'They fought? Why?' Akash was surprised.

'Actually, you know, we were all annoyed that Samar was not spending too much time with us.'

'But he has a girlfriend, Jess. So what's the big deal?'

'I know, but I guess we felt neglected. Imly and I were furious because of Dhruv's behaviour.'

I told him everything that happened that day.

'What an idiot!' Akash said and sat next to me. 'You should have told me this before, Jessi!'

'I don't know. I broke down and…'

'For that bugger? Please don't give him so much attention.'

'You know! I just want my gang back. I miss Terrance. I hope things are fine next week when I go to school.'

'Jessi, why do you worry so much? You have sad eyes.'

I laughed at what he said, 'What do you mean?'

'I mean, you are beautiful, but you are tragic kind of beautiful.'

'Really? You think so, Akash?'

'I think so, yes!' And we laughed together.

Remember one thing! The world does not go around the way we expect it to.'

'That's the sad part, I know.' I frowned at the thought.

This time he laughed it out and caressed my hair with his hand. This was the first time I had seen Akash using his touch to express.

He got up to reach his study desk. He picked up a gold plated tulip from his desk and placed it in my hands, 'Jessi, this is for you.'

'What's this for?'

'I got it from Amsterdam, and I just felt like giving it to you.' He stood in front of me. I felt strange, so I got up to leave.

'You are leaving?'

'Yeah.'

'I have Zumba in the evenings.' We were standing facing each other, and I looked him in the eyes.

'Right now? I mean it's going to be 7?'

'Oh! It's 7?'

He smiled, and I smiled. I wanted this moment to be with Samar. But it was Akash in front of me. Suddenly, Akash held my face and cupped my chin with his hands. He kissed me softly; his lips met mine; my arms around his neck and his hands now resting on my waist. He pushed me to the couch as we kept kissing. It was an awesome feeling, and I was totally into it until Dhruv's words resonated in my ears.

'Stop!' I pushed him back. I picked up my bag and left his house immediately.

#TheBoysRoomSaga

'Oh gosh! I don't want this to happen. I must intervene, but how do I enter the boys' washroom?'

Samar and Terrance were fighting in the boy's room.

'Hey, what's happening, Jessi? What is this chaos all about?' Yana asked.

'This is getting out of our hands.' Yana was worried for Samar.

There was an announcement, *Good morning. The Assembly is taking place in another five minutes. Please proceed towards the assembly area. Thank you.*

'Leave it, Jessi. We have to go inside,' Yana told me.

'Are you sure? The assembly is in another five minutes, Yana.'

'Chuck that. This is more important.'

'Okay,' I replied, and we both went inside the boys' room.

Terrance was holding Samar's collar, and his mouth was bleeding.

'What the hell do you think you both are doing?' Yana shouted at both of them.

Both of them remained silent.

'What drama is this? We are friends and you guys are abusing each other and fighting like animals!' I told both of them.

'What was the problem?' Yana asked Samar.

'Nothing, don't bother.' Samar tried to deviate from the topic. I knew the reason, but I decided to remain silent.

'Whatever, just end this fight, okay!' Yana warned Terrance and Samar.

'May I know what's happening here?' The counsellor was standing at the door.

'Sir, nothing, just...' Terrance tried to explain, but the counsellor interrupted him.

'I want all four of you in the counselling room, immediately.' He left after saying this.

'Oh gosh, we are in trouble now.' Yana frowned.

'Don't worry; I will handle it,' Samar assured her.

'It's all because of you both! What was the need for the fight?' Yana screamed at Samar.

'Let's go now. We have to give smart answers. Everybody on the same page.' Terrance said and looked at Samar, but Samar ignored him and went out of the boys' room first. I entered the counsellor room first and all three of them were standing behind me.

'Go, Jessi. You go first,' Yana said.

I sighed and entered the room.

'Sir.' My body shook a little by unknown nervousness.

'Please take a seat. Where are your friends?'

'Err... They are here at the door with me.'

'Do you need a formal invitation?' The counsellor raised his voice towards the door, and Yana closed the door as soon as we all stood next to the counsellor's table.

'First of all, I would like to know what were you both doing in the boy's washroom?'

'Sir, Samar and Terrance were in trouble. The sophomore boys were bullying them both.' Yana coughed and made up this one.

'Who were those guys?' The counsellor looked straight in Samar's eyes. But, Samar and Terrance kept looking at the floor tiles. No one replied as they had no answers.

'Hey, you! What's up with this blood on your mouth?' The counsellor was finally turning towards Terrance as he got up from his chair.

'Sir, some guy from twelfth grade but I don't know his name,' Terrance said, trying hard to escape the counsellor's eyes at him.

'And may I know why they bullied you? I mean, tell me the whole story. Fast! I don't like one-liners! Can you both girls leave now? I would call you if I need any answers.'

As soon as the counsellor said that, Yana and I scurried away to our home room.

◆

'These boys were too much! I just hope they are out of that room soon,' Yana said as we walked in the hallways.

'We need to fix this. The gang can't go on like this. We need to make a truce between them.'

'You are right. Let's meet this evening at my place. Samar can come to my place and you can bring Terrence,' Yana said and I agreed.

I went towards the locker area to take my books out for the home room class. I opened my locker and saw Akash. His eyes met mine and I felt a flutter in my heart. I smiled and he smiled.

I was experiencing a different feeling. Is it a new love?

'Hey, you okay?' he asked while still taking out something from his locker.

'Yeah, all good!' I said.

'See you then.' He locked his stuff and then cupped my chin with one hand. Then, he went straight towards the home room after giving me an infectious smile which made me blush.

When I went inside the class, I couldn't find either Terrance or Samar. I asked Yana, and she shrugged. 'I hope they are not suspended or something.'

'Oh, gosh!' I replied.

Mrs Nayanthara started reading a case study based on the book *Animal Farm* by George Orwell.

'We will discuss the corrupting influence of power. How many of you have read this book?' I felt conscious as I saw from the corner of my eyes that Akash was looking at me.

Soon, the day ended. I didn't know the whereabouts of Samar and Terrance. I knew that I had to resolve this war.

#StudentExchangeProgram

'Hey, you in a saree?' I exclaimed as I saw Yana standing on the stage in the assembly area.

'I am welcoming the foreign students. Mrs Nayanthara said we have to be in traditional attire because we have to display our culture. You know the principal said that the most beautiful girl in the school would welcome the foreign students.'

'By the way, I really can't find Samar and Terrance?'

'Don't look around. They are not coming,' Yana said.

'Why?' I asked.

'Because they have been suspended for three days.'

'Oh, man, I knew this.' Imly shook her head in disbelief.

After our brief interaction with Yana, we went towards our class queue.

'Hey look! Somebody is watching you,' Imly elbowed me.

I spotted Akash and he waved. I waved back.

'Jessi! Go and meet him. Just initiate small talk, for god's sake. Oh wait, he is coming here. All the best!'

'Hey, Jess!'

'Hey, Akash!'

'I have been assigned to give foreign students a tour of our environment-class. You can join in.'

'Sure, I would love to.'

'Okay, after the assembly, the foreign students are all assigned a host family to take care of them. We have to take the four students from Malaysia. Involve them in recreation and maybe play table tennis with them. What do you say?'

'Sounds good.' I blushed.

◆

After the assembly, I started walking towards the environment room as I had a pending project to finish.

I picked up the glass bottle that Akash worked on and observed it for a few minutes.

'Knock knock,' Akash said.

'Hey!'

'You are in love with this?' He winked at me and I blushed.

'Yeah, I guess so.'

'Tomorrow is a show. A carnival of sorts, a parade… *mardi gras* style…'

'Oh!' I turned the hot glue gun on for the project.

'And a theatre play I guess?' Akash said while holding the bottle for me while I put the glue on it.

'Oh yeah! I forgot to tell you that. We are practising *Little Women* today,' I said.

'Oh! So are you going to stay back after school hours?'

'Yes.' I smiled and pressed the glue on the beads and then pasted them one by one on the glass bottle.

'Hey, Akash!' I jumped as I got an interesting idea to share with him. 'Why don't you act in the play with us?'

'Me?' he asked surprisingly.

'Yeah, you!'

'You gotta be kidding me. I can't act.'

'But you can try. See Laurie in the play is missing, and we are having a hard time searching for one. Can you be Laurie please?' I literally begged.

'I don't know Jessi,' he hesitated, but I was adamant.

'Okay, if you say so…' After much persuasion, he finally gave in.

'Yay! You are so pricey!' I jumped in joy. I thought I would hug him instantly, but I held myself.

◆

The practice room was full of students, and their usual chattering continued for a long time. There were photographers, make-up artists and students who had to perform, all geared up for the next day's theatre play.

Little Women was one of my favourite novels so far and I was lucky I got to play Jo in the play.

'So who's playing Laurie now?' the play director asked.

'Don't worry. The head boy is coming in a couple of minutes,' I assured her.

'Okay, I want only the performers to be here for now. The lighting and sound crew and other members can join us around 3:30 p.m.?' she announced, and only six people were left in that room. I took a sigh of relief.

Akash entered the room with a coffee in his hand.

'For you,' he handed it over to me.

I grabbed the coffee mug from him and smiled.

'I have never seen this side of yours.' I winked at him, and he just smiled while looking at me.

#TimeForTheLittle WomenPlay

A large crowd had gathered in the multi-purpose hall, including the foreign exchange students in the front row.

I was a little nervous, so was Akash. Ananya announced the play title and gave a brief description of the author and the book. We started enacting and Akash was beyond my expectations. My heartbeat became faster than ever as my next scene was with him.

As per the scene requirements, I was supposed to disappear into a curtained closet and then, come face to face with Laurie.

'I am sorry I didn't realise anyone was here,' I blurted out.

He laughed and said, 'Don't mind me. Stay if you like.'

'Wouldn't I bother you?'

'Not at all! I came here because I don't know many people and felt a little strange by myself.'

'So did I,' I said awkwardly, for we both had to act shy.

'Well, thank you for the Christmas dinner.' I managed to say my line.

'That was my grandfather's idea. Uh, how is your cat, Miss March?'

'Very well, thank you, Mr Laurence; but my name is Jo, not Miss March.'

'Very well, I am Laurie, not Mr Laurence.'

'Would you dance?'

I held his hand, and we managed to dance down the little stage.

Soon, the play got over. The audience applauded and the whole cast and crew appeared on the stage. Akash and I smiled at each other from a distance. He was so marvellous, for a moment I thought he was the real Laurie.

'You know what? Samar and Terrance came from the fields and went back!' Yana said.

'Like seriously?' I raised my eyebrows.

'Yeah, and they watched your show with Mr head boy!' She giggled.

'Oh, okay, I will call him.' I didn't want Yana to sniff my newborn feelings for Akash.

◆

At night, when I was reading my book after dinner, a WhatsApp notification popped up on my screen.

Akash: Hey, sup?

I kept the book on the side table and lied down on my stomach.

Jessi: Hey, nothing much. Just reading a book.

Akash: Okay, dinner?

Jessi: Done! Yours?
Akash: Done.
After a brief pause, he typed again.
Akash: I can't stop thinking about you! I feel close to you. I feel that I know you for so long.
Jessi: And what is the reason to feel that way?
Akash: I don't know.
Jessi: I will see you at school tomorrow.
Akash: Hey, wait! Can we bunk school tomorrow?
The bunking thing reminded me of Dhruv.
Jessi: No.
Akash: Okay, can we go to the Waffle House across the street after school?
Jessi: Yeah, after school sounds cool.

#DayTing

'And this is what we call infinity.' I heard Mrs Nayanthara say that as I entered the class.

I spotted Samar sitting next to Yana and Terrance sitting alone, so I went and kept my bag next to Terrance's seat.

While the class was struggling with Mrs Nayanthara's unit of inquiry, Akash entered the class, all drenched in the rain. He looked handsome. I looked at Samar and he winked at me. I gave him a polite smile.

Imly was sitting behind me and she whispered in my ear, 'What's cooking babes?'

'I am supposed to meet him at the Waffle House after school,' I whispered back.

She giggled, and I shushed her.

'I can't keep calm. I am so excited.'

'Shhh!' Mrs Nayanthara shushed us, and the bell rang for the twenty-minute break.

'Okay, I hope everyone is ready to go to Rishikesh on Saturday? Please keep some warm clothes and jackets, sun hats, some games,' Mrs Nayanthara announced before leaving.

I saw Akash waiting for me. I told him to meet me after ten minutes next to the basketball court.

'Hey dude, you back?' Akash shook hands with Samar.

'Yeah…'

'Welcome back!'

'Asshole!' I heard Samar swearing once Akash left the class.

'Samar, shut up!' I snapped back at him.

He just shrugged.

'We are going to the coffee room, you want to join Jess?' Samar wanted to change the topic.

'No, I am good.'

'Okay, catch you later then.'

◆

On my way to the basketball court, Dhruv struck in my way.

'Hey Jessi, what's up?'

I ignored him, but the school's music teacher was with him, so I had to stop and first greet the teacher and then reply to him.

'I am good. How are you?' I said sarcastically.

'I am great, as always. Are you going to the basketball court?' He smirked, and I understood what he meant. I noticed that Akash was already there in the court and looking at his watch, time and again. I decided to go back to the class instead of the basketball court.

The rain had stopped, but the scent of the soil filled my soul. I had to tell Monty about some extra class after school, and he would have to leave with Mahesh after school got over.

When it was the bus's leaving time, I walked towards the Waffle House. It started drizzling when I reached the Waffle House around 3 p.m. There was no one inside, except a guy sitting with his laptop who didn't even lift his head.

I spotted Akash sitting close to the window. I kept my bag on the chair and patted his shoulder.

'Hey, Akash!'

'Hey!'

'Looking for me?' I asked.

'Yup, you didn't come to the basketball court?'

'I got busy,' I lied.

'Or you forgot?' He smiled and held my hand. I felt strange.

'What, tell me?' He caressed my hand with his thumb.

'Nothing! I am just nervous.' I thought the butterflies were going to explode in my stomach.

He left my hand and smiled. He sat back and relaxed on his chair while scanning the menu card.

'What would you like to have?'

'Chocolate milkshake,' I muttered.

He gestured to the waiter, and ordered, 'One chocolate milkshake for ma'am and coke for me.'

'So, all set for the trip?' He looked at me, and our eyes met for a single second. I blinked and looked at the crew working behind the counter.

'Yeah, almost, and you?' I managed to say.

'Oh! Lots to be packed. Why don't you come to my house and help me with the packing?'

I felt embarrassed as immediately the memories of our last meeting at his house came up and stood in front of me, just like the waiter holding our order.

'Uh, I have some dinner plans with my family. I am sure you would do a good job of packing and stuff.'

There was silence for a couple of seconds, and then I said, 'How's your dad doing?'

'Same old thing! Same old alcohol,' he scoffed.

I pressed my lips and looked at him, then took a sip of my milkshake.

My phone buzzed. It was Samar.

'Hey,'

'Hey, Jess! What's up?'

'Nothing, you say.'

'Hey, Yana and I are going to Baskin-Robbins for ice cream, you wanna join in? Should be fun.'

'Actually I am at the Waffle House right now.' My speech broke suddenly.

'What? Waffle House? Next to the school? What are you doing there? And with whom?'

'I am with Akash,' I muttered.

'What? You promised me that you are going to stay away from him. You cried because of him! You remember that, Jessi?' He screamed from the other end.

I got up and went towards the door, 'I did not cry because of him, I cried because of Dhruv.' I was careful enough to not let my voice reach Akash.

'Jessi, you didn't tell me?' Samar's voice was loud.

'You know what! I will wait for you and Akash for ice-creams, okay?'

'Yeah! Okay!'

I went back to my milk shake and Akash.

'Hey, everything all right?' he asked.

'Yeah! It was Samar...he wants me to join him for ice cream. Would you come with me to Baskin-Robbins?'

After a little thought, he agreed, 'Okay, sounds good.'

'We still have an hour.' I smiled at him.

I bit my nail, but he immediately took my finger out of my mouth and said, 'I think, you have been a spoilt brat since childhood?'

'Not at all! And what made you think that?' I laughed.

'Just like that. Sometimes, I feel like pampering you. I want to know how much pampering you have already gone through in your life, and how much I can do if I am allowed to?' He smiled.

'Umm...Akash we are just good friends, and you are special, but...'

'Hey, stop! Don't you dare friend-zone me, Jessi!' He held my hand and looked straight into my eyes.

'What do you mean?'

'Jessi, I have a special place for you in my heart. Let's go now!' He got up and paid the bill.

◆

Akash booked a cab to take us to Baskin-Robbins. We were quiet; Akash fiddled with his phone and I looked outside.

When we reached Baskin-Robbins, Akash told the cab driver to stop.

As we entered, it started to pour heavily.

We found Samar, Yana and Imly sitting cosily around a table next to the window and giggling.

'Hey everyone,' I stood there with Akash, and no one replied as if I had given them some kind of electric shock. Only Imly greeted us, that too after a minute.

Samar kept quiet, but shook hands with Akash and kept looking at me after every few minutes, as if judging my emotions and my feelings for Akash. After Akash and I shared two scoops of the Mississippi mud ice cream, he left as he got a call from his dad. The rest of us went back in Samar's car.

'See you tomorrow! Be on time for the outstation trip and call me if you need some help packing.' I bid him goodbye before sitting in Samar's car.

'Sure, if everything goes well, I might join you tomorrow. I hope everything goes well.' Akash left after that.

Samar did not ask me anything about Akash, but I knew from his anxiety and his cold behaviour that he would discuss Akash soon!

#RishikeshDiaries

When Mahesh pulled over our car to the parking area of the school, I saw a white Mercedes-Benz bus. Some of my classmates were boarding it.

'Whoa!' I exclaimed as I got out of my car. Mahesh took my luggage and kept it next to the bus. Imly ran towards me when she saw me, and we hugged each other in excitement.

'I am so excited, Jessi. This coach looks cool, isn't it?'

'Yeah! Totally!' I pressed her hands in assurance.

'Hey, did you see Akash?'

'No, I didn't, but Samar and Yana have already boarded the bus.'

'Let me call him.'

'What happened? Is he not coming?'

'I don't know. I need to call him right now.'

I hurriedly dialled Akash's number, but he didn't pick up. I dialled it again and again, until Mrs Nayanthara gestured to everyone to board the bus.

'Oh god!' I whined as I boarded the bus. I saw Samar and Yana sitting on the back seat and laughing with other classmates. Dhruv was sitting on the front seat and I gave him a stare. He didn't say a word.

I trudged ahead on the aisle and found an empty window seat in the middle area of the bus. Samar came to me, 'Hey, why are you sitting here? Come join us, we all will sit together.' He held my arm, but I resisted.

'Uh, no…I mean, I will join you in a while. I need time to settle down.' I sighed.

He just shrugged.

I really needed to know why Akash didn't tell me that he won't be coming? What could have gone wrong? What if he never wanted to come in the first place? He should have told me yesterday. I was getting anxiety pangs.

The engine of the bus started. My heart sank deeper as the bus started moving slowly. My eyes were filled with tears.

I decided to distract myself and sat with Terrance because it'd been days I didn't talk to him after his fight with Samar in the boy's room.

'Please stop the bus for a moment!' Mrs Nayanthara called out to the sports teacher Mr Dharmesh. He told the driver to stop the bus as some student had just arrived.

I cocked my head on my left to see who it was.

'Oh my god!' I muttered when I saw Akash thanking Mrs Nayanthara. I sighed and waited for him to walk to where I was standing. I wanted him to see me. But he seemed busy, greeting everyone and apologising for the delay. I pressed my knuckles.

'Excuse me, everyone, please sit down. The bus is going to move now!' Mr Dharmesh raised his voice to a merry pitch.

'Come on! Look at me!' I pressed my lips while muttering.

Finally, Akash spotted me, and a broad smile spread on my face. I gestured to him with my hand to the seat where I was sitting, and he nodded in return.

He kept his backpack up in the baggage area. I could smell his cologne; a heady mix of woody, spicy and musky and then laughed at myself again.

'What's up?' He smiled and touched my cheek.

'Where were you and why didn't you pick up my phone?'

He sighed for a moment and then he turned towards me. 'I don't want to start this trip with you by discussing the details of what happened at my house today after breakfast. How my dad scowled at me!'

'What?'

'I was disappointed by his behaviour, Jess.' He gave a dismissive shrug.

I tried to change the topic as it was making him upset, which I never wanted. I tried to cheer him up.

'You know what? I love the way you call me Jess and not Jessi!' I muttered to him in a voice so low, it was a miracle he heard me.

He smiled finally. I looked out of the window. There was an air of excitement on the bus. Will and other girls from a different band were singing. I could hear Yana's irksome girlfriend's giggling at the back.

'Do you like it here? I mean with me?' Akash asked me after he heard the whole bus singing and laughing, though I was sitting with him.

'Why do you ask?' I spoke softly.

'Because I don't sing and laugh like all the other guys and I don't even do Halloween dance.'

'But you write poems and play piano. You are different. That's what I like about you. I can see numerous versions of Akash within you; some are even dormant,' I pressed his hand, and he tightened the grip. No more words were exchanged. I loved the warmth of his hands.

Laughter broke out in the back row of the bus. Yana, Imly and Samar were having a ball.

I spotted Terrance getting up from his seat, coming towards me. I promised myself to make it work on this trip between him and Samar.

'Hey, Jessi!' he said and forced himself a smile.

'Hey Terrance, can we go and join our gang at the back?'

A smirk made its way across Terrance's face. He looked at me with astonishment as if I had committed some crime by asking him this simple question. I had to accept his silence.

The bus trudged along the ring road and the heavy traffic, while we sat and enjoyed the sing-song atmosphere inside the bus.

Mr Dharmesh announced that the bus would stop at a nearby restaurant for some breakfast. The bus slowed down, I took out my hat, and we waited for our turn to get down from the bus. I didn't wait for Samar and Yana, and that irked them.

'I am going to the girl's room. I will see you inside the cafe.'

'Okay, I will wait for you here,' Akash said.

'Sure, I will be back soon.'

By the time I came back, I found Samar standing next to Akash and arguing. I quickened my steps to listen to their conversation, but Samar left by the time I came.

'Why was he here?'

'Yeah, he wanted to know the same.' Akash scoffed.

'What do you mean?'

'You ask him. He sounded as if you are his girlfriend!'

'Okay chill!'

'Let's go.'

We went inside the cafe to have some snacks. Ananya came to chat with Akash, and they went on for a couple of minutes. I spotted Terrance talking on the phone, sitting in a corner seat.

'Akash, I will be right back.'

'Okay.' Akash nodded without looking at me and continued his talk with Ananya. I went and sat right next to Terrance.

'Hey.'

'Hey,' he replied without looking at me and just browsed his phone.

'Do you mind leaving your phone for a minute?'

'Okay, cool.' Terrance kept the phone down.

'What is happening, Terrance? Let's forget the differences and be friends.'

'We *are* friends, Jessi.'

'I am talking about Samar.'

'You need to ask him about the same.'

'I will! But I wanted to come to you first and talk to you.'

'Jessi, look! He thinks I made fun of his girlfriend. Do you think I would ever do that?'

'Look, I don't know who made fun of whom, but I don't like the fact that we don't hang out anymore! I mean, just look at us!'

There was silence and for a brief moment, then Terrance smiled at me. I could see he missed the time together. I didn't waste a single second of that moment and grabbed his arm and led him towards Samar and Yana.

'Jessi! What? I mean, what you up to, girl?'

'Don't say anything. We are all going to talk.'

◆

Samar and Yana were sharing a Hamburger and a coke.

'Hey, Jessi,' Samar offered me a seat.

'Yana, what do you think? Terrance and Samar should make up?' I put my elbows on the table.

Yana immediately replied, 'Of course, Jessi. Even Samar misses Terrance!'

Samar scoffed and got up. For a moment, we all thought he was going to bash him again. Imly also joined and stood frozen. We were all waiting for the next scene as if watching a movie and guessing what would happen next.

In an instant, Samar grabbed Terrance by his shirt and hugged him. Terrance hugged him back tightly.

'Whoa! That is awesome.'

As soon as I said that, they both let go of each other.

No words were exchanged between them. It was a clear sign that the boys had called it a truce.

'Wait guys, I will order some food for all of us from my side.' Terrance was so excited to be back that he went on treating everyone.

'I will come along. I need a red bull,' Yana accompanied Terrance to the cash desk.

Samar grabbed that moment to vent out his anger against Akash, 'Hey, Jessi…what's up with you and Akash? Why are you with that dork?'

'Samar, we like each other.'

'Are you sure? Is he honest with you?'

'What do you mean?' I scrunched my eyes at him.

'I mean, do you even know him? His dad is a drunkard, and he has a broken family.'

'How does that make him a guy bad?'

'I am not saying he is bad, but he is distressed in life, and when you get along with distressed people, they end up making you get involved in all their troubles.'

'So?' I asked surprised.

'So, you end up only thinking about them and their miseries and not about yourself.'

'Well, first of all, he is not miserable. He is perfect in every sense of the word.'

That did not go well with Samar, and he scoffed but kept quiet.

I looked at Akash and Ananya. They were still talking and I couldn't help getting jealous. I noticed Ananya was wearing a super short skirt and she kept folding her leg and then unfolding them. I thought it was to gain some attention from Akash.

'I don't want this new episode in my life now,' I murmured to myself.

'What did you say?' Samar cocked his head.

'Uh…nothing,' I wanted to run away from him to get to that table and slap Ananya.

'Where are you looking? I am talking to you, Jessi!' He sulked.

'That the head boy and the head girl are talking!' I made an angry face.

'How does it even matter?'

'It does!'

Terrance and Yana arrived with lots of cold drinks, waffles and chips.

'Hey, cheers to our friendship! Woohoo!'

I was happy to see the old Terrance back!

#ChroniclesOfMovingOn

The bus trudged along the beautiful landscape, and after hours of grey roads and traffic signs, the landscape changed to blue, brown and green. The mountains mesmerised us, and the chirpy songs continued.

Soon, we reached our hotel. It was an overcast sky, and we excitedly de-boarded the bus and checked into the hotel. It was still late afternoon. The teachers assigned us our rooms, and we got ready for a lovely evening. The wind was chilly, and the air was damp. The sunset painted the whole atmosphere in hues of orange and crimson.

I looked at Akash's face and his tan complexion was deluged in the shades of orange and crimson. Soon it was dark and the hotel guys arranged for some wood for bonfire and camping tents.

'Come on, students! Let's pitch the tents. We need teams.' Mr Dharmesh called out to everyone.

The teams were made, and I was with Terrance and Will. My heart sank when Ananya and Akash were made to pitch their tent together.

'I can't take this anymore,' I told Imly while hammering the screw to the ground.

'What?' Imly stopped for a minute and asked me.

'The fact that Akash and Ananya are together.'

'They are not together Jessi! They are just pitching the tent together.'

'I know that, but I hate it. I mean it could have been me with Akash.'

'Jessi, you are always so jealous. You have to trust him.'

'I do, but I don't trust Ananya.'

'Doesn't matter as long as you invest your trust in Akash, Ananya doesn't stand a chance.'

I looked at Imly with so much love and respect that I wanted to hug her, but I told her instead, 'You know what? You are the best friend I could ever have.'

It gets dark rather early in the mountains. Samar and Yana prepared the wood for the bonfire to be lit when it's dark, which was sooner than we had expected.

The hotel arranged for some barbecue snacks and soup for everyone. We sat around the bonfire and played games, still in teams, though. Small plumes of fire rising from the bonfire looked magical.

Akash came and sat next to me when Samar was singing a song and playing his guitar. His face glowed in the light of the bonfire, and I was sure he wanted to kiss me. Imly was right.We need to put in a lot of trust in the person we love.

Akash whispered something in my ears that I couldn't understand amidst the sound of the music and the guitar.

'I am sorry, what did you just say?' I smiled at him.

'I said, I love you.'

'Oh, I thought…' I had no words and I could feel the heat flashed on my face.

'Do you?' he whispered again.

'Akash,' I giggled.

'Do you?' he asked again, and I just nodded.

He sighed for a moment and zipped his jacket up and chewed his gum. Then he poked me with his elbow, and I poked him back, and we giggled silently.

'This is the last trip of the year before the winter vacations begin, so let's make the most of it and enjoy,' Mrs Nayanthara was a happy woman that day, and she kept humming the songs that the students sang and snapped her fingers in between.

After the celebration, the food, the barbecue and the excitement, we all retired to our rooms. I was sharing the room with Imly. She changed into a night-suit that had watermelons painted all over.

'Hey let's watch some Netflix?' Imly suggested.

'I have some episodes left for *Riverdale*.'

'Mine too. Let's watch it together. I got my laptop.'

'You log in; I will make some cup noodles.'

'That is so awesome. I have been craving the same since morning.'

'See, now you have it.'

And as we sat to watch *Riverdale* on Netflix, our room's doorbell rang. I peeped through the hole and found Samar's face. I held the door before I opened it.

'I know why he is here,' I whispered.

'Who is at the door?' Imly slurped the noodles.

'It's Samar. I will be back soon. I know he wants to talk about Akash.'

'Is he mad?' Imly scrunched her eyes through her spectacles.

'Shh, don't!' I gestured to her to keep quiet.

'Okay.'

He smiled as soon as I opened the door, 'Hi.'

'Hey, what's up?' I asked.

'Can we talk?'

'Yeah.'

We went outside for a stroll. There was nothing except the empty tents, the cold wood, and the leftover coal where the barbecue machine was kept. The air was damp and windy. Sharp winds gusted in from the nearby lofty mountains and streams. I put the hood on my head and my hands in my jacket.

'Listen, Jessi,' he initiated the talk.

'Tell me, Samar,' I giggled, slightly chattering my teeth.

'This is no time for a joke,' Samar sighed.

'Wait! Are you going to tell me something serious?' I stopped and looked at him.

'Yes, only if you listen to me.Jessi, I feel that you deserve a better guy. I have always felt that way.'

'Hey, stop! Now don't tell me that Akash is not good enough for me. I don't want to hear anything like that.' I folded my hands and made a stern expression.

'I am not saying anything about him. All I am saying is that you deserve a better guy.'

'Oh? And who is that better guy?'

'That guy is me, Jessi!'

I opened my mouth in disbelief, 'Are you out of your mind? You and Yana are a thing, and the entire school knows about you both. Who are you fooling?' I looked straight into his eyes in a fit of rage.

'Relax Jessi! Yana and I are not in a serious relationship. We are dating casually, and she is not the kind of girl I would get serious with.'

'What do you mean?' I was so angry at the fact that all those months I spent in Delhi thinking that they both were a serious relationship was a lie. And now, this man whom I adored so much ever since I was a teenager was telling me that he had found his perfect girl in me.

It is so confusing. What should I do now? I have moved on. I love Akash more than anything else in this world.

Oh gosh! I felt I was going to faint right in the middle of those barbecue coal remnants.

'I mean to say that I always found you too perfect for me. Yana is never even close to that,' he said hesitantly.

'But you never showed those feelings before? You always disconnected my phone when Yana called you in the middle of our phone calls, and despite being online on WhatsApp, you never replied to my messages? Also, when I messaged you on Instagram, you didn't bother to reply to me, but kept liking Yana's pictures. I mean, I was hurt!' I blurted out everything that was there in my heart.

'Oh my god! Jessi! You never told me these things before. Why on earth would you be interested in stalking me on social media?' He didn't believe what I said.

'I liked you, Samar. But you were always with Yana, and I am not the kind of person who would come in between a happy couple.'

'We are not a couple, but you could have told me whatever you felt.'

'You never bothered to reply to me. Just check your inbox right now.'

There was a brief pause. Then, I continued.

'Look, I have moved on Samar and I love Akash very much. He loves me too!'

'Does he reply to you on time?' He joked.

'We don't communicate on Instagram or WhatsApp. We talk in real because our love is real,' I clarified, still folding my hands.

'And you think that your love for him will stay forever?' he asked sarcastically.

'I trust him.'

'Jessi! I don't want you to get hurt.'

'Why are you so worried for me now? Just go back to Yana. You shouldn't even be here with me.'

'Okay! But think about it, Jessi. You are too innocent, and things aren't the same as they appear.'

'I want to take my chances, Samar.'

There were no more words exchanged. I had a tear in my eyes for all the emotions that were in there for Samar.

Still, my heart decided that I didn't want to go back to that miserable me who used to wait endlessly for Samar's text messages. Akash was enough for me now. I wiped my tears when he was gone.

#InTheWoods

The next morning brought a lot of much-needed sunshine. It was time we all were ready to go for some adventure. The team from the White Water Rafting company was at our resort, making some announcements.

We all gathered around the area where we set the camps and listened to the team.

'Our rafting trip starts at 1:30 p.m. The minimum weight requirement is 13 kilograms, and the maximum is one-hundred kilograms. I hope everyone present here is eligible?'

We all split into peals of laughter.

'Sir, Terrance is underweight,' Imly pointed towards Terrance.

'Shut up, you nerd! You are overweight.' Terrance was quick to reply and everyone chuckled aloud.

'Okay students, I know you are very excited for river rafting but there are a few points to remember. Please carry an extra pair of shorts. We will provide you with life jackets and headgear. Wearing safety gear is compulsory. Please don't wear fancy shoes, no flip flops, no *chappals*, just sneakers or if you have river shoes. Carry sunscreen and sunglasses. We provide straps for your sunglasses so that you don't lose them. Remember, sunburns can happen fast at a higher elevation and can be severe. Sunburns or hypothermia are no fun, so use sunscreen. We will guide you as to how to hold the paddle and everything once we reach there. Now, let's leave in another thirty minutes. Please prepare yourself. We will meet in the area where your bus is parked.'

When we reached the parking lot and started boarding, Yana confronted me, 'Hey!'

'Hey, Yana. What's up?' My head started spinning because I didn't get good vibes from her hello.

'What is it happening between you and Samar?' She threw the question directly without even looking at who was around us.

'Let's talk inside the bus. There are people boarding,' I replied. I kept calm and boarded the bus. She followed me to the last seat. Samar had not yet boarded the bus and she wanted to end this discussion as quickly as possible.

'What do you want to hear Yana? There is nothing between us?'

'Don't lie to me. Samar is getting mad about you and one of my friends told me she saw Samar and you in the camping area last night talking for a long time.'

'Does that prove anything?' I asked.

'Yes, it does. Samar told me he was sleeping because he was tired, but he was with you!'

'I don't know why he lied, but we just talked like friends.'

'Don't you lie, Jessi! Just because you don't have anyone in your life, that doesn't mean that you can eye my boyfriend!'

'Stop it, Yana! Don't you dare speak to me like that!'

'Why not? When you can dare to speak to my boyfriend!' She spewed so much anger.

We both spotted Samar boarding the bus, and we soon realised that other students were looking at us and our high-pitched volumes. So we parted ways and went to different seats to sit. I sat with Akash on the very first seat, and Samar sat with Terrance. Yana was more fumed because Samar didn't sit with her. She sulked and did not speak to anyone for a long time.

◆

When we reached the White Waters Rafting place, we were awed by the beauty of the Ganges. For a moment, I completely forgot about Samar and Yana.

'This looks cool,' I told Akash.

'Wow, man! This place is just so beautiful,' Akash said. He was equally amazed by the natural landscape and the beauty of the white waters.

The guide who was trained at CPR and first-aid made a couple of safety announcements. 'Our team will now start to hand over paddle jackets to all of you. Please listen to the commands carefully. Never stand up on a moving current. Watch out for rocks coming from downstream.'

River rafting was new to all of us, and we had so much fun rolling down the stream in a raft that was wobbly like hell.

I held Akash and he held me. Suddenly, we both started giggling, and we found this whole adventure a bit too much for our quiet personalities.

Terrance started singing a song, and suddenly while the raft was moving ahead, due to the heavy work of the white river, the shape of our raft was perpendicular. Everybody shrieked, and the guide told us not to panic as it was expected, 'Just keep calm and get a grip of yourself.'

He kept yelling this, but we couldn't concentrate. We were so scared. Suddenly, the sound of the song faded away and only we could hear the stream and the waves and the voice of the guide. I looked around and couldn't find Terrance.

'Oh my god! It seems he is in trouble. I guess his foot is stuck in that rock.'

The guide immediately jumped into the water and took him out. They took him onshore. Meanwhile, our raft went ahead, overtaking the small and large rocks. I was screaming and felt like puking. Akash held the barf bag in front of me and I did puke a little. I felt nervous and embarrassed. I could just hear somebody say 'Terrance is safe' before I passed out.

When I woke up, I was in my room, and Akash and Imly were there with me.

'What?' I woke up with a jerk as if not expecting all that.

'You okay?' Akash rushed to my side of the bed.

'Yeah, I am okay,'

'You still look a little perturbed though,' Akash held my hand while Imly got some water for me.

'I think it was too much for me.' I bit my lower lip and could feel that my lips were dry because of dehydration. I picked up the glass from Imly who caressed my head while sitting next to me.

'How's Terrance?' I suddenly remembered about him.

'He is fine, and he has gone with everyone for trekking,' Imly said.

'And you guys didn't go?'

Imly sat next to me and said, 'I fibbed to the teacher that I got a sprain in my leg although all I want to do right now is to click some incredible photographs of the landscape outside. I got my DSLR and want to use the bokeh effect that I learnt in a short photography course that I did last month.'

'Wow, that is awesome.' Akash smiled at her.

'Okay, so now I take leave from here.' She took her camera bag and went outside.

'See you,' my voice was a little hoarse from the cold weather.

'You should drink more water, Jess.' He drew some water from the kettle and handed over the glass to me.

'Thank you for being here with me, Akash.'

'Don't be formal Jess.' He kissed me on my lips, slowly capturing the essence and feeling my lips. He held my waist when my lips started responding to his. That went on for a few seconds, and then I broke the kiss. I held his face with my hands and looked into his eyes.Then, we kissed again, and different sensations engulfed my body. I felt warm and secure.

'You want to go out?' he asked me.

'If you want to.' I winked.

'Let's go.' He handed me my jacket and filled up a water bottle for me from the kettle.

'Where are we going?' I asked while I locked the door.

'In the woods!' He smiled as he zipped up his jacket.

We spotted Mr Andrew in the corridor.

'Oh man, what is he doing here?' Akash said.

'Leave my hand, Akash,' I whispered, and he immediately distanced himself from me.

We kept our heads down as we were approaching our teacher who kept staring at us as he was coming to our side. Soon, he was gone from sight.

We talked as we walked towards the woods. The scented pine engulfed the atmosphere. We could hear some birds chirping. The mountains in the background looked magical.

'It is cold,' I shivered.

'Told you! You didn't even want to wear your cap,' he laughed, and I held him by his arm.

'You need my jacket?' He offered and started to zip it down.

'No, I am good.' I held him close, and he caressed my hair. He put some strands behind my ear and then kissed right there.

'I love you Akash.'

'I love you more.'

We kept walking and admiring nature, the mountains and the landscape.

'You passed out on a raft?' He laughed out so loudly that his voice started echoing in the woods.

'Shut up!' I chuckled along.

'I mean seriously? Girls pass out in the bar washrooms and puke and you? In a raft? You are amazing.' He touched my cheek with his cold hands.

'Ouch! Don't do that. Your hands are cold.' We snuggled closer and held each other's hands as we kept walking.

It was dead silent. Now even birds were not chirping. Not a word anywhere! Just us! We didn't say anything for some time, and then we heard some footsteps. For a moment, we thought that it was the sound of the crumbling of leaves under our feet, but we stopped and still felt like somebody was following us. We waited next to a young cherry tree. The sound had stopped. We looked at each other.

'Let's go back. It's getting dark,' I murmured.

'Oh my god, there is a wolf, Jessi!' Akash held me even closer now.

'Where?' I panicked.

'It's coming towards us.'

'Let's run.'

'We can't! We are stuck now,' he said.

'Akash, I am terrified.' I started to cry when he started laughing and I looked at him in sheer shock.

'I was just kidding, babe,' he chuckled and released my hold and instead lifted me in his arms.

'Here is the wolf and now there is no escape.'

'My werewolf!' I slapped on his cheek lightly, and we laughed out.

'Okay, let's go back. Seriously, it's getting dark.'

'Hey, shhh! I saw somebody familiar there.' He pointed out at a stark tree nearby,

'No more jokes, Akash!'

'Wait right here, Jess. I will be back.'

'Hey,' by the time I said that, he was already walking.

I waited there, shivering. I tried to scrunch my eyes to see who was standing there. The boy was wearing a red checked shirt with jeans and a black jacket. It was at a distance, though. And then I saw Akash holding his jacket collar and thrashing him on the grass.

'Oh my god, Akash!' I ran but froze when I saw Dhruv standing there. His nose was bleeding. Akash punched his face again before he ran away.

'He was stalking us?' I was huffing when I said that. 'Is he gone?'

'Yeah, I told him I am gonna report him,' Akash said furiously.

'You shouldn't have thrashed him.' I frowned, still holding on to his jacket as we sloped downhill.

'For the love of my life, I can do anything! Becoming Mohammad Ali is one of them.'

'For now, I would love to see you in poet mode, so carry on.' I giggled.

'You want to climb on my back, Jess?'

And without waiting or my reply, he lifted my hands while kneeling with his back facing me. I climbed at his back and put my hands around his neck.

'Continue...'

'Some say the world will end in ice...'

I gave him a warm hug which melted his anger. Like always, his embrace gave me warmth and comfort.

The sun was about to set, leaving a shameless vermilion around us. The wind was quiet and brilliant.

◆

At the camp

'Yana, listen to me, babe.' Samar held her hand.

'Stop! Just stop, Samar! I don't want to discuss this further. How dare you?' Yana yelled at Samar.

'I didn't do anything…'

'Oh, you know what? Just leave!'

'But listen to me once, babe…I love you. You know that.'

'You love Jessi. You just told Imly. I heard you!'

Samar didn't say anything in his defence. Yana stood, folding her arms, her lips quivering from the cold, and her eyes were wet.

#EverythingEverything

'Students! Tomorrow your review exams begin, and I want full attendance. Please prepare thoroughly and enjoy your Christmas holidays,' Mrs Nayanthara announced when the bell rang for the twenty-minute coffee break.

The students rushed to the canteen and locker rooms, but Imly and I went straight to the little coffee room.

'I have no idea what it would be like,' I told Imly.

'What do you mean?'

'I mean the coffee room without Yana and Samar?'

'I know it sucks. But believe me! You have other things to be happy about.'

'Like what?'

'Akash?' She winked.

'Of course, but I need my gang back!'

'Let's be hopeful,' Imly said.

As we entered the coffee room, Samar was there playing his guitar and Terrance tapping on the table. Only Yana was not there. We filled our cups with coffee and sat down next to Terrance.

Samar ignored me for a while and kept playing his guitar.

'Why aren't you with Akash today?' Samar finally spoke.

'He is playing basketball, and I wanted to be with my friends,' I looked straight into his eyes, but he shrugged his shoulder.

'Aren't couples supposed to be with each other all the time?'

'Only if they are insecure,' I replied.

'I see,' he responded.

'You didn't patch up with Yana?' I asked, breaking the silence.

He ignored my question, left the guitar on the corner of a wall and left the room without any explanation.

◆

'Monty, can you lower down the volume of your Xbox? I need to study. I have an exam tomorrow!' I scolded him in a tone that I had never used on him before. Just then my phone screen blinked. It was a message notification from Samar.

It said, *I am feeling very weird*. I sighed. I took my books and phone and went to my bedroom instead.

I typed *Hey, what's wrong?*

He replied immediately, *I don't know...but I feel like talking to someone.*

'What a narcissist! Now that he didn't have Yana to talk with, he wanted to talk to me?'

I replied, *Okay, we can chat here if you want.*

Samar texted, *But I want to talk on the phone.*

I can't, because mom can come here anytime with my dinner.

You can go out and talk for a while? He sent the message with a wink emoji.

I thought for a moment. He could have done the same when I wanted to talk to him so badly. Did he make that effort for me? No!

Um...you know what? I have to hit the books now! We will talk in school. Bye!

I put my phone in flight mode and opened my book.

◆

Next day in school, Yana sat next to me while the teacher was distributing the assessment sheets to us. It was the exam day, and I was quite nervous. On top of that, I didn't have a clue why Yana chose to sit with me. She didn't smile at me or even looked at me.

'What do you think of yourself?' Suddenly she started talking as soon after one hour had passed. I was writing my exam, but I replied to her.

'What do you mean? If you think I am responsible for your break-up, then you are wrong!'

'I don't trust you anymore,' she said spitefully.

'You don't have to, and I don't think I need to explain myself.'

After a moment of stillness, we both wrote our assessment, and after fifteen minutes she blasted again. 'You know what? There is a huge difference between you and me! You don't even deserve him.'

I scoffed and then got up from my seat. I handed over the A4 sheets to the teacher and went out of the class.

I went to the washroom and sat there for ten minutes. I reflected on a lot of things that were bugging me.

I washed my face and went to the basketball court. As usual, Akash was practising there.

'Hey,' he said.

Should I tell him or should I tell him not? Why bother him with unnecessary stuff. I thought and just sat on the steps to watch him play. 'Hey!' I replied.

He kept playing, and I kept watching.

'That bugger is suspended for three days.'

'I know, Dhruv deserved it!' I replied.

'Yeah, totally babes!' He wiped the sweat on his forehead and then sat next to me.

'You want to go and watch a movie after school?'

'Which one?' I finally smiled.

'*Everything Everything*! It's a nice one! You want to go with me?'

'Yeah okay! I loved the book, so I guess I would like the movie too!'

'Okay then, see you in the evening. How did your assessment go?'

'It went well. Text me. I have to go now. I have to look for Monty and leave for home.'

'Okay, will text you.'

◆

'Mom, Are you there?' I threw my bag on the couch and switched on the television. There was no response. Monty went inside the kitchen to check.

'Amma is unwell.' Lakshmi came with a glass of water. I switched off the television and rushed to granny's room.

'What happened?' I opened the door where I saw mom sitting next to granny while a doctor was examining her.

'Her saturation went low all of a sudden, so she is being put on oxygen now.' My mom said, and I held her hand. I looked at my frail grandmother, and tried to call her, 'Granny? It's me, Jessi.' There was no response. I felt quite sad as I sat next to her, caressing her forehead. Her mouth was open as she was inhaling the artificial oxygen.

My mom paid the doctor his visiting charges and told me to eat my lunch as she would be busy with granny.

I came out of the room and saw grandad, who caressed my head with his hand. We stood there and I kept thinking about him too. No matter how stressed he was, he still wanted to assure me that everything would be all right.

'She will be fine! Don't worry. It's old age, that's it. One day, we all have to go through this,' he said and went inside granny's room after I gave him a nod.

I called Akash, post my lunch when I went to my room.

'Hey Akash!'

'Hey!'

'You still in school?'

'Yeah, we had a match.'

'When are you leaving for home?'

'In some time, Jess.'

'You don't like going back to your dad, right?'

'No, I had a match, that's why.'

'Okay, my granny is unwell. She is on artificial oxygen.'

'Oh, I hope she feels better soon, Jess.'

'Yeah.'

'So, we are going to the movie, right?'

'Yeah, there is nothing to worry about. I will talk to mom after some time and then text you?'

'I will come to your house around 6 p.m. See you!'

◆

In the evening, Akash entered my house as I hurried down the stairs. He was holding a bunch of pink carnations.

I blushed with embarrassment. My mom warmly greeted him. I didn't want any more embarrassing so I picked up my sling bag from the couch and decided to leave the house as soon as possible.

Before I could do that, Akash called my mom and requested, 'Mrs Sethi! If you allow, may I please take your beautiful daughter out for a movie tonight? We will be back on time.'

'Go ahead and enjoy yourself! And yeah, be back on time.'

'Thanks, Mrs Sethi.'

When my mom turned back to leave, he called her again.

'Mrs Sethi?'

'Yes?'

'Can I meet granny? I got some flowers for her.'

'Sure, please come with me.' And she led him to granny's room. I was surprised, but quietly followed them.

Akash stood next to granny and placed the pink carnations in her left hand and told her, 'Hi granny, I am Akash, Jessi's friend and I hope you feel better soon. These flowers are for you. I will see you soon.' This time, granny's eyes were open, and she tried to say something. She raised her hand to bless Akash.

◆

After I sat in Akash's car and passed the dimly lit tree-lined lanes, I popped the question, 'I thought, you got those flowers for me?'

He didn't say anything, just increased the volume of the radio.

We reached the cinema and bought a big box of popcorn and iced coffee. And after our popcorn finished, Akash took out a red rose from his jacket pocket and handed it over to me. I kissed him on his cheek, and he grabbed me by the waist and kissed me passionately on my lips.

'I love you.'

'I love you more.' And he kissed me again as he said that.

It was a memorable day, watching my favourite kind of movie with the one I love.

#ExcitedForTheYearEnd

Finally, the exams were over. We were discussing the plans for the graduation party. The sophomores were planning a prom style party with us so we had to find a partner to dance with. There was a meeting in the music room for the eleventh and twelfth graders to make the final event as memorable as possible.

'Who's going to give the graduation speech?' Ananya asked as she stood right next to Akash.

'I can do that,' I immediately decided to volunteer.

'I can do that too!' Yana raised her hand too.

'Okay, cool. You both can do it,' Ananya wrote the sequence of events in her notebook and Akash looked on.

'Akash, what do you suggest more?' she asked as if he was the only deciding factor there.

'I don't know. Let's ask everyone around,' he said as he fiddled with his phone. He then made eye contact with me and finally, I smiled.

'Let's keep a dress code for the party,' Yana, being the stylist that she is, was quick to bring some ideas.

'Give some ideas. You are a stylist.' Bill looked at her while checking some strings on his cello.

'Sure, I would say, let's keep it formal as most schools do. The boys wear black suits and girls formal gowns?'

'Yeah, that would be nice. Too good Yana!' Most of the girls agreed to the dress code. The boys had issues with whatever the dress code was because they don't care as long as they are having fun.

'Who's going to be our DJ?' Samar popped the right question.

'Of course, Khalid. Who else?' Bill laughed out loud.

'Yeah, we're done then,' Samar said while looking at me. I ignored his gaze.

As we went out to go to the cafeteria for some lunch, Samar followed Imly and me, 'Jessi, wait!'

We turned around and stood there, waiting for Samar to talk.

'I will meet you in the cafeteria, Jessi.' Imly understood the intensity of the situation and left.

'Why are you doing this to me, Jessi?'

'What I am doing?'

'Ignoring me!'

'I am not ignoring you. Your girlfriend is after my life. She holds me responsible for your break-up?'

'What did she tell you?'

'Nothing, seriously! I don't even want to discuss this anymore. I gotta go!'

'And you blocked me on your Instagram?'

'I deleted my account because I have no time for social media. It's a delusional world.' I walked away as soon as I saw Yana coming towards us.

◆

Back at home, granny's health was getting worse day after day. I was apprehensive about her. I sat with her most of the time and read my books

In another week, the school would be closed for the Christmas holidays and would open only on 7 January. Then, the session would end with the graduation party on 15 January.

I was wondering how time flew from the day I arrived from London! Akash and I went on dates and spent the lovely Christmas looking at the lightings and decorations around the city. We decided to end the year with clubbing at a nightclub.

That night, I dressed in my little black off-shoulder dress and used my curling tong to give waves to my #PlainJaneLook.

I sat on the willow wicker chair on the porch and waited for Akash. I spotted Samar taking out his car from the driveway and speeding through the narrow lane. I was wondering what he was up to? Just then, a message popped on my phone screen, 'I am outside your house.'

'Mom, I am leaving.' I picked up my clutch from the glass table and opened the gate.

'Okay honey, don't be late,' my mom said as she came to close the gate.

Akash was mesmerized when he saw me. As we passed the tree-lined lanes of my neighbourhood, I spotted Yana walking her dog. She didn't notice me.

‘That was Yana?’ Akash immediately noticed her.

‘Yeah.’

‘What’s up with her? She is not going out with Samar?’

‘They broke up.’

‘Really? What happened?’

‘Just leave it for now.’

◆

We had some fun time partying together and welcoming the New Year. Akash dropped me home at 12:30 a.m. I slept like a log until the ring of my phone woke me up. That was Akash. I looked at the wall clock and it was already 6:00 a.m.

What? Why is he calling me at this time?

I picked up the phone.

‘Hello.’

‘Jessi, I can’t live with this man anymore,’ Akash’s voice was low.

‘Wait…what happened?’

‘He was drunk; he hit me last night and started using abusive language. I can’t take it anymore, Jess.’

‘Where are you right now?’

‘I am at 24 seven.’

‘Oh, Akash, you better go home. Everything will be alright.’ I said in my sleepiest tone.

‘No, Jess, nothing will be fine. I am not going back to that house again.’

‘Are you kidding me? Okay, book a cab and come to M main near my house! Let’s talk it out.’

‘No, I don’t want to bother you. I will handle it myself. I will call you later.’

'Listen...' But he had already hung up. I tried calling him again, but his phone was switched off.

◆

Two days later

I never had anything going good for more than a month! There was no school, no studies, so where was I supposed to spend my time? I didn't want to go to Zumba. I only visited granny twice a day. Her deteriorating condition made me more depressed and I couldn't stay any longer and returned to my room every time.

It'd been two days but Akash hadn't called me. I needed a friend badly. I dialled Samar's number but then, disconnected even before the first ring. I felt alone again in life

I decided to go to his house the next day, but before that, I again tried my luck calling him. Fortunately, it rang, and he picked up at the second ring.

'Wait, I will just come to your house, Jess,' Akash hung up without me even uttering a word.

He came to my place in the evening. He entered my room after greeting my mom and visiting my granny. He got another bunch of pink carnations for granny. I closed the room purposely after he was there.

'What happened?'

'Can we go for a walk outside, Jess?'

'Yeah sure, please give me a minute.'

We hurried towards the outside lane without letting mom ask us questions. We stayed quiet for a minute until we reached the park. When we finished crossing it, he said, 'I am leaving Jess.'

I was dumbstruck. I popped the question without letting him speak anything further, 'Are you breaking up with me, Akash?'

'Jess, I mean to say that I am leaving the country this weekend. I am going to my brother's.'

'Why?'

'That night when I dropped you home, my dad and I had a bad fight. He got somebody home, and I couldn't take it. I abused him, and he did the same.'

'Oh!' I was shocked.

'So, he called up my brother, and I didn't even know he had already arranged for my tickets the week before. He doesn't want me to stay with him and disturb his life.'

'So you are not coming back anytime soon?'

'I don't think so.'

'And what about us?'

'Jess, you need to move on. I can't drag you in my problems. I care for you.'

There was a silence for some time.

'I don't know what to say.' I turned towards my house and started walking.

'Hey, I am sorry,' Akash was at a distance now.

'When is your flight?'

'Sunday.'

'Have a safe one!' I opened my house gate without looking back and went straight to my room.

◆

I felt terrible for Akash, but I felt worse for myself. Unable to sleep, I called up him. It was 3:00 a.m. He picked up the phone.

'Akash?'

'Yeah, Jess.'

'I hate feeling like this,' I cried.

'Shh! Stop crying. It's the worst for me. Just imagine me staying in this house after all that has happened with me.'

'I can't understand all that. I just know that I can't live without you.'

'Jess, there is nothing in the world that is irreplaceable, you know that?'

'You are Akash, you are!'

'No, I am not.'

'Just get lost then.' I hung up the phone, as anger dominated my brain.

I went back to my balcony to calm down. The cold was bitter. The January wind pierced my mind, froze my emotions, but I stayed there watching the stars that glowed above me. The smell of the wintry breeze made me sleep somehow, there on the floor.

The sun rays woke me up, and I squinted my eyes to open them. I was astonished to see that my legs felt numb, and my eyes hurt after incessant crying last night.

I kept it to myself most of the day. I didn't even visit granny. I disconnected Imly's call, knowing well that she was the only person whom I could talk with. The reality was that even she couldn't replace Akash for me. Nobody could.

◆

I was lying down on my bed, and it was pitch dark. I didn't know how it became so dark all of a sudden. I was wondering why I was not able to open my eyes even if I tried hard to do so. Then, I tried to move my legs, but I was horrified to realise that I couldn't move them too! Did someone tie me up? Only my brain was working, and I couldn't feel anything until someone held my toes and pressed them hard.

I cried in pain, but my voice didn't come out of my mouth. I shrieked in horror when I saw a blank face standing right in front of me! I woke up, startled! It was a bad dream, and I was sweating profusely.

I threw the blanket off from my body and switched on the lamp next to my bed. Then I looked at the wall clock that showed 3:20 a.m. I realised I couldn't sleep anymore.

I dialled Akash, but he didn't pick up. His flight was scheduled that evening. I crawled out of my bed, rubbing my eyes and went downstairs to granny's room. I sat with her for some time; just watching her pale face and the oxygen mask on her mouth. She was breathing slowly. Suddenly, I had an urge to cry beside her. I kept my head on her shoulder and talked to her, 'Granny, I am devastated. Nothing good happens to me. I end up losing everything in life. What should I do? Please talk to me. I miss talking to you, granny. I need you. I am devastated. Help me, please!'

And then the sobbing continued for a couple of minutes till I noticed the saturation monitor beeping. I checked her pulse and the oxygen level. The oxygen level dropped to 50, and she started having difficulty breathing. I held her hand, but then the oxygen level dropped to 40.

'Oh god!' I hurried my steps outside her room, woke up, mom and dad.

'Mom, granny is having a hard time breathing.'

Mom and dad hurried to her room and called an ambulance. Dad increased the oxygen level and rubbed the soles of her feet.

'Maa! Maa!' He called out, but granny didn't respond. The ambulance came in ten minutes, and granny was transported to the nearest hospital, which was just two kilometres away. Dad and mom went with her, and I looked at the empty bed, her shawl lying on the floor. The crease on her bed made me cry again. I cried loudly at that time.

What if she doesn't come back? I would lose everything! Her CD player was intact, and I clicked the play button. *Hanuman Chalisa* played.

I never prayed much in my life, but that day, I joined my hands and prayed to god to let her stay for some more time.

Little did I know I was asking for too much! My phone vibrator buzzed.

'Yeah mom, is everything okay?' I was already crying.

'The hospital confirmed that she has passed away, honey. You take care. We will bring her home in an hour. Please inform Monty.'

At that moment, I felt the whole earth underneath my feet just opening away in a crater. I was going inside an endless void.

#Void

My legs felt shaky as I went to Monty's room upstairs. I shook him up from his sleep.

'What?' He got up with a jerk.

I cleared my throat and tried to speak, 'Granny is no more, Monty.'

'What? What happened to her?'

'Wait, she is not downstairs. We called an ambulance. She is in the hospital right now.'

Monty cried a lot in his room, and then we hugged each other tightly for a couple of minutes. We had to support each other during this tough time.

◆

As Monty and I stood there amongst the hundreds of people that turned up for my grandmother's last rites, I found Samar standing right next to my mom and dad, putting sandalwood sticks on her pyre. We had eye contact for a moment, and then I saw him coming close to us. He hugged Monty and offered his condolences to us.

'I am so sorry for granny.'

'Thanks.' I managed to say. I realised my lips were dry, and my eyes sore. I didn't want to face Samar anymore, so I excused myself to drink some water from a nearby tap. I spotted Imly, Yana and Terrance entering the crematorium. Each one hugged me, and I cried my heart out.

Yana hugged me even tighter, 'I am sorry for everything Jessi!' I guess she wanted to apologise for misbehaving with me the other day in school. I forgave her immediately as I understood that friendship is more important than any relationship in the world.

Terrance and Yana went to pay their final tributes by offering sandalwood and rose petals to granny while Imly stayed with me and cornered me to show someone. 'He came. Look, there he is! He told me everything, even when you didn't.'

I hugged Imly tighter. 'I am so sorry Imly. I am devastated. First he and then this! I don't know what is happening?'

She comforted me and patted my back.

I saw Akash leave after offering his condolences to my parents. He made a second of eye contact with me before leaving. It filled my eyes again. Imly caressed my back, and I nodded.

The thing about people leaving us is that they never come back! Some might come back, but not in the same way that they entered your life.

◆

One month later

When school reopened in February, everything felt different. I didn't know why. The students were the same. The excitement on their faces was the same, the hallways filled with their chitter-chatter. And the echoing of the assembly announcements!

The basketball court was empty. I sighed and moved on to the animal gym corner. I offered some biscuits to the dogs there. Terrance patted me on my back.

'Oh my god, for a moment I thought it was...'

'It was?'

'Oh! Nothing.'

'Let's go to class. We need to discuss our graduation party.'

'The date has been set and the dress code finalised. Now, all you have to do is to find a partner for yourself. The next fifteen days are going to be fun finding someone you love. Woo!' Ananya said. Everyone cheered in excitement, except me.

Imly told me in the hallways next to the locker rooms that Samar had a talk with Yana in that coffee room and she guessed that they finally made up with each other.

'So that they can have each other as partners at the prom,' I pursed my lips.

'Whatever,' Imly shrugged.

'Whatever! I am not coming to the prom so that you know.'

'What? Why? You know that I am covering the event. I am the official photographer of the event,' she got angry at me.

'Imly, you know what I went through.'

'Find yourself a partner, Jessi. Move on in your life. What's gone is gone! You look like a body without soul!'

'What's gone is not gone from my mind!' I banged the locker door and walked away towards the cafeteria.

'How many days would you sulk? Weeks? Months?' she said as I continued walking away.

'I don't know. It's not over for me yet.' My voice was comparatively high at that time, and I was wondering why kids in the hallway were watching me with their eyebrows shot up.

As I passed through the music room the next day, I heard everyone practising for the prom dance. I stood for ten minutes while a sophomore guy and a girl practised dancing to Ed Sheeran's song. I watched them with great joy.

Can we incarnate somebody's lost love in another person? I mean when we lose someone, are we able to receive what we lost? Ever?

So many questions and no valid answers. I entered the classroom. They announced another guy with the highest scores in the whole session as the next head boy.

I felt that knot coming back again in my stomach, and I excused myself to rush towards the girl's room. I puked until my lungs felt nothing but void.

◆

For two days, I didn't go to school at all. The preparations for the prom that I found to be joyous before soon turned against me. I felt terrible for myself! I felt weak! I was sleeping in my home for two days. Mom got worried and came to ask me if everything was okay. She knew I missed granny a lot. I did! That was true.

The third day when I didn't turn up to school, Imly visited me in the evening. She told my mom about the prom, so mom came rushing to my room with the ballroom dress that she had worn when she was a teenager.

The magnificent blue looked beautiful. But I had no inclination to wear that without having Akash as a partner. Mom displayed that dress on a wooden hanger in front of my bed every day. It was in front of me until the day of the prom.

Imly came to pick me up on the prom day. I was sleeping in my pyjamas. She shook me, literally. She had her camera and tripod.

'So, have you decided to disappoint your friends on this day? Jessi! It's such a big day for all of us! Look, everyone's got together. Yana and Samar patched up. Terrance and Samar are again friends!'

'I told you I can't go. Please go and enjoy it.'

'So we mean nothing to you?'

'That's not what I said.'

'But that's how you are behaving.'

And then, in a fraction of a second, she got up from my bed and brought that blue ornate dress and displayed it right in front of my face.

'Wear it for yourself, Jessi. Sometimes, you don't need a partner. All you need is a friend.'

'Imly...'

'Now go and change. I will not budge from here till I take you to the prom.'

'Okay!' I managed hard to move my body, took the dress from her hands and slowly paced towards the washroom.

When we came down from the stairs, mom and dad were delighted to see me.

'You look just like your mom,' dad cupped my chin.

'I am so happy,' my mom cried, watching me.

'Mom, relax! I don't want you to have a migraine!' I rolled my eyes at her, and she hugged me tightly.

#GraduationParty

The track *Say Something* by Justin Timberlake welcomed us as we entered the prom venue. It was a vibrant ambience. I spotted Terrance standing next to the DJ. He wore a bandana and looked very different. We smiled at each other, and then he waved.

'Hi, Jessi,' I turned around and found Samar standing there in a gorgeous black suit.

'Hi, Samar.'

'You look good, Jessi.'

'Thanks.'

'I am sorry about Akash and you,' he hesitated to talk to me.

'It's okay. You don't need to be sorry.' I bit my lower lip.

'Hey, you guys stand together and I click a picture?' Imly tried to change the topic.

'Sure, let me get Yana here,' Samar disappeared quickly in the crowd and then came back holding Yana's waist. She looked gorgeous in her Fuchsia gown and ultimate curls and metallic eye makeup. Imly clicked us as we posed for the picture.

I excused myself and went to Terrance. I asked him to play a couple of Marshmallow songs. As I was standing on the stage with him, I realised how girls and boys were enjoying themselves; dancing around, having a ball.

I checked my phone, but there was no call from Akash. I didn't want to stay in the party for a long time, but my name was already announced for the opening speech. And I decided that I would leave before the graduation speeches by the sophomores and the valedictorian.

◆

Ananya announced my name, and I nervously climbed the stage after getting down from the DJ console podium.

I cleared my throat, took a deep breath and adjusted my mic.

There is no greater honour than delivering a speech in front of my peers, teachers, family and friends on this special day. I welcome you all, and I am delighted to share common emotions in this room. It was a special year for me. I didn't know how the year flew by!

I never thought I would be able to cope up in Delhi, but I adjusted more than I had expected. Life gives you reasons to enjoy, love, understand each other, and we should live it to the fullest. It's been a year full of great happenings, music festivals, outstation trips, making close friends, learning with teachers, especially Mrs Nayanthara. You are truly an inspiration for all of us. Thank you so much for everything!

The twelfth graders who are graduating now, I wish them all the very best for their future endeavours. I am sure you all are excited to start a new chapter in your life, so write your own story and make sure it's a good one!'

The room filled with a light applause, and Mrs Nayanthara nodded with a smile.

I walked down, and everyone just kept cheering and clapping as I walked past everyone, including Samar, Yana and Terrance. Imly gave me thumbs up and clicked my pictures. Everyone cheered, the music began, and I could see everyone dancing as I headed towards the exit gate. To be a part of those celebrations meant more misery to me and missing Akash more than I intended to.

I wanted to run away from everything at that moment. I changed my clothes to regular jeans and a white T-shirt and booked an Uber to the school. The office was open, but the school was closed as it was a Saturday. I paced my steps towards the basketball court. I imagined him there, playing basketball and remembering the first time I met him when I was about to get the hit from the ball on my head, and he caught it on time. I smiled at the thought. Then, I went to the environment class where his projects were lying everywhere. I moved my eyes. I touched everything his hands had touched in that room; plants, old bottles, the broken cage, the cardboard boxes that he got from a scrap seller.

'Everything is incomplete without you here...even me Akash!' I whispered to myself. I cried as I sat on the floor. My lips were parched like a desert with no rain and my hands dusty handling the cartons and other recycled things. I was wondering where to go next because nothing felt like home since he left.

#Serendipidity

'Hey Jess, why did you leave early from the prom? We were looking for you all over the place!' Terrance stopped me in the hallways after two days when we all met in the school.

'I was not well. I went back home,' I told him while taking out my books from the locker.

'Jessi, stop lying at least! We are all your friends,' Imly shouted at me for the first time.

I kept quiet as I had nothing to say.

'Jessi, we are a gang, remember?' Yana cocked her head and smiled.

'Thank you everyone, but I will have to deal with my issues on my own,' I replied while still trying to figure out how to get out of that locker room space without being answerable to anyone.

'Listen, Jessi, if you want to be on your own, it is fine with us. But don't be shocked when we walk past you without even noticing you in future!' Imly snapped back at me.

I sighed and kept my French notes in the locker. As I locked it and turned, I found that they had already left. It was just me and the eerie silence of the hallway.

I held my notebooks under my folded arms, passed through a lot of lockers, including Akash's. I stood there for a moment and touched it.

'What are you doing here, checking my locker?' I panicked as a voice startled me from. I turned around and found Akash standing right next to my locker. He posted a sticky note on my locker. I went back to my locker to read what it said.

I am not going back now. Nothing is more important than you. I missed you so much that I am ready to live with my dad here.

He stood there, smiling at me, tilting his head.

'Oh my god! Seriously? Is this you?' I dropped my books and hugged him.

'There are cameras here otherwise I would have kissed you right now!' He cupped my chin with his warm hands. Then, he picked up the books that I had accidentally dropped and placed them in my hands.

'Serendipity it is!' Imly and Terrance shrieked in excitement.

'Yes, it is! Most definitely it is!' I laughed as we hugged each other again.

Epilogue

Samar started by tapping on the desk. 'The loopy day is over. Stand up, shake up and mixup!'

Yana's girl friends continued by moving their shoulder blades. 'And we sing, and we whoop it up!'

Yana contributed as she flossed. 'Let's get this bread honey.'

'Just spent my friend's money,' Imly added.

'Start up, warm-up and just party baby,' Terrance sang.

'You know my future is no more hazy,' I sang while performing the Orange Justice.

'For you are my leading lady,' Akash sang.

'Conquer within which hides everything; open up and fly with your wings,' Mrs Nayanthara said with a smile.